P9-CRK-385

JASON PINTER

Published by Sourcebooks Jabberwocky, an imprint of Sourcebooks, Inc.
P.O. Box 4410, Naperville, Illinois 60567–4410
(630) 961-3900
Fax: (630) 961-2168
www.jabberwockykids.com

Library of Congress Cataloging-in-Publication data is on file with the publisher.

Source of Production: Webcom, Toronto, Canada
Date of Production: April 2012
Run Number: 17360

Printed and bound in Canada.
WC 10 9 8 7 6 5 4 3 2

To Brian Jacques, Terry Brooks, and Stephen King,
who showed me that discovering amazing new
worlds is as easy as turning the page

PROLOGUE

To Who It May Concern

(Wait...is it "who" or "whom"? Ugh, I can never remember. If I live long enough, remind me to ask Mr. Statler in homeroom tomorrow.)

My name is Ezekiel J. Bartholomew. I figure my parents gave me that name because they were really popular and had a lot of friends growing up and by naming me Zeke it would balance out our family's popularity. Most kids in my school have names like Tom or Mike or Freddie or Bill. In fact, I've never met another Ezekiel in my life. Most of my regular friends call me Zeke, so I guess you can call me that too. I say "regular" friends because I have another friend too. My friend will soon call me Sea Otter. I know, I know. The name Sea Otter doesn't exactly strike fear into the hearts of my enemies, but you'll learn who my *other* friend is and why I'm called Sea Otter very shortly. In the end it will all make sense.

When I was in the third grade, my gym teacher wrote on my report card: "Zeke is medium everything." So after everything that happened, even after everything was explained to me, I've often asked myself: how could a twelve-year-old "medium everything" become the most wanted kid in the world? I'm still not totally sure. But what I do know is this: if you're reading this letter, he's found me. The most dangerous person in the world. My nemesis. (Or the person reading this is my dad, and you snooped around my room when I've told you a million times that it's totally off limits when I'm not home. So if you're my dad, ignore everything I'm about to say and stop reading right now. It's just your silly, daydreaming son, Zeke, pretending to be a superspy again. But if this isn't my dad, then you'd better listen closely, because the fate of the world is at stake.)

You might think everything I'm about to tell you is a big lie. "Zeke loves to make up exciting adventures because he's never going to have any of his own!" you might say. Or, "There goes Zeke again, Zeke the daydreamer, the joke of an inventor, thinking he's some sort of kick-butt spy, when in reality I'd pick an inflatable mattress over him to be on my dodgeball team." I wouldn't blame you for thinking that. My fourth-grade English teacher, Ms. Wilderman, wrote that my short stories "lack creativity." See, right from the mouth of a teaching professional. I'm not creative enough to make up what I'm about to tell you even if I wanted to. I've never been creative on paper, but I also never thought my creativity might save the world.

So I can understand why you might not believe me. But I promise you that this is all true.

If you're reading this, it means he's still out there. The most dangerous person in the world. He knows I'm still alive. But I also know that he knows I'm still alive. I'm not sure why he wants me to know he's still alive, unless he just wants me to be pee-my-pants scared over the possibility of him coming for me, but to be honest, after everything that's happened, I say *bring it on.*

So this is the truth. This is how the fate of the world fell into the hands of an unimportant dorky kid from nowheresville. This is how it all began. But before I start, you need to know his name. The true identity of my nemesis. My foe. The person who will stop at anything to kill me.

So whatever you do, if you find this note, know that he is out there. And he is...*uh-oh, I can hear my dad coming up the stairs. But this letter isn't ready yet. I'd better hide it where nobody will ever find it…*

EITHER THE BEST DAY OF MY LIFE OR THE WORST

Once there was a boy destined for greatness. He had a very distinctive scar, and anyone who saw it immediately knew who he was and how he got it. He possessed amazing magical powers and was fated to save the world. He lived in a wondrous realm, full of adventure and derring-do, and every day brought fantastical quests, creatures that seemed to have leaped from dreams, prophecies that would change the course of millions of lives.

This boy's name was known throughout his realm, and ours, and it is still spoken by children and adults alike. Books were written about this boy. Movies were made about him and his friends. His life is known by everyone with a pulse.

I am *not* that boy.

My name is Zeke Bartholomew, and the only thing I

have in common with "you know who" is an identifiable scar. Only mine wasn't carved by some evil wizard...mine was caused through sheer stupidity. Let me explain.

When I was seven, I tried to create a zip line. I'd seen it in a spy movie once, the hero skimming effortlessly along a razor-thin wire from a skyscraper to the street while a fire raged below him, firing at bad guys with precision aim. Looked easy enough, and I was a fairly smart kid, so I understood the physics behind it.

That zip line was the first cold slap in my face letting me know that I wasn't an action hero, just a regular kid.

When my dad wasn't looking, I climbed out through the attic window with a fifty-foot piece of rope I'd found in a dumpster. I'd also found a discarded bike handlebar in the trash, and what was one person's trash was another person's treasure.

I tossed one end of the rope to my best friend, Kyle Quint. Kyle tied that end to a tree while I secured the other around the chimney. Once both sides were taut, I yelled to Kyle.

"Ready?"

"Ready, Zeke!"

I swung the handlebar over the rope, making sure the

zip line fit snugly between the metal. I tugged it. The contraption felt good. I gave Kyle a thumbs-up.

"Go for it, Zeke!"

I gripped the handlebar, got a running start, and lifted my feet off the ground. At first it was incredible. I was sailing through the air, just like James Bond might have done.

"It's working!" I yelled to Kyle. "We did it!"

And that's when the handlebar detached from the rope. In my excitement, I'd neglected to secure the underside of the handlebar. Not very James Bondian. Before I knew it, I was upside down, hurtling through the air. But rather than in a cool, downward fashion that would have left me standing triumphantly, I was plunging straight down into a tree.

I smacked against the branches, felt something tear at my face, then tumbled to the ground. That's the last thing I remembered before waking up in the hospital with a broken arm and fifteen stitches where they sewed my upper lip back together.

Now, five years later, my arm has healed. And if you look closely you can still see the scar on my lip. At the time, that zip-line adventure was the most exciting thing that ever happened to me. Unlike "that" boy (you know, the one with the cool forehead scar and magical powers) a failed zip line was the height of my adventures. So I lived through books and movies and TV shows. Wanting to be that boy everyone knew. The boy who could save lives and change the world. But it wasn't meant to be.

Until the day *he* moved in next door. My own "he who shall not be named." And from that day forward, my life was never the same.

It all started on a day like any other. The sun rose. I had waffles for breakfast. And I caught my dad absently scratching his butt while eating a bowl of cereal. It was a rerun of pretty much every day of my life.

Except for the moving vans.

"You have got to be kidding me," I said, peering through the fence in my front yard. My best friend, Kyle, was kneeling next to me. I couldn't believe what I was seeing. It didn't seem possible. I couldn't tell if this would be the best day or my life or the worst.

"Some real estate broker must have a really good sense of humor, Kyle," I said. "Because I'm pretty sure a family of spies just moved into the house next door to me."

Kyle looked at me, in a way that said, *Here we go again.*

"Sure," he said. "Just like that tribe of gypsies living beneath the community swimming pool that turned out to be a knitting group."

"They looked suspicious," I replied.

"Or the gang of motorcycle hooligans plotting to poison the town's water supply."

"In my defense, he had a bicycle and was doing something to the water that wasn't right."

"Come on, man. Let it go. It's a family with a few cool cars. If you're lucky, their kids will have all the new video games."

I wanted to argue with Kyle, because I couldn't shake that feeling. There they were. A family of three unloading box after box from a car the size of the school gym. A woman and man who appeared to be married, and the silhouette of another person still inside the car. I couldn't tell who the third person was or how old he or she was, but the person didn't appear to be in a hurry to help. The man and woman weren't unloading regular cardboard boxes. You know, the kind with masking tape peeling off of them and big, sloppily written words on the sides that say things like CAROLINE—OLD BABY CLOTHES and RALPH—BOWLING TROPHIES.

No, this family was unloading huge aluminum containers onto dollies with the kind of delicacy and precision usually reserved for plutonium. I looked at my jeans with the ketchup stain on the right knee, my sneakers with the rubber soles coming loose. I didn't own anything worthy of being transported inside a cool-looking bomb-proof container.

"Those containers are rust-proof," I said to Kyle. "Whatever's in there must be important."

"You know there's a rational explanation for all of this. Maybe it's like a collection of really old baseball cards or family albums."

"It's definitely not family albums," I said as the man gingerly placed a crate onto a dolly, biting his lip as he did so.

My family had lived at 5 Sunnyvale Drive all of my twelve years. The house next door had been unoccupied for the last three, ever since the Wickershams moved to New York City when Mr. Wickersham got a job at an advertising firm (or as my dad put it, he "went off to be the Grand Pooh-bah at some hoity-toity ivory tower. Hmph").

I was friends with their son, Wally Wickersham, and

it sucked when they left, because that meant Kyle Quint was my only friend left on Sunnyvale Drive. Kyle's a great guy and all, but he's six-foot-four, and Wally and I could only beat him in basketball when we played two-on-one. And even then Wally had to cling onto Kyle's leg while I made a layup.

Kyle is the tallest kid in the seventh grade by almost a foot. We met in kindergarten when we were both the shortest kids in our grade. Since then he's grown at double the speed of everybody else. He's one of the best athletes in the class and always gets picked first or second in pick-up games. But he's also one of the shyest kids you'll ever meet. On the court he's a six-four demon, swatting shots and running like a llama. Or a gazelle. One of the two, I'm not good with animals. But off the court he blends into the background and is forgotten about as soon as the game ends.

Over the last few years, I'd gotten used to the house next door—7 Sunnyvale Drive—being empty. On Halloween it was the only house that didn't get egged or covered in toilet paper. What's the fun in TP'ing a house if nobody lives there to get all upset?

But then one night the moving vans came. They showed

up around ten o'clock. A pretty strange time to move in. The moving men were all dressed in black jumpsuits and wearing dark baseball caps. They all had earpieces attached to cords that disappeared into their black pants. These guys definitely didn't want anybody paying attention to them. I watched the whole thing through the window in my bedroom, thinking there was something weird happening on Sunnyvale Drive.

Then around eight o'clock the next morning, one huge black SUV pulled up to the house. Kyle had come over for our daily walk to the bus stop. We watched as a man got out of the car. He was about my dad's age—well, only if my dad looked like he could finish a triathlon in his sleep, used a pound of Jell-O to hold his hair in place, and had a jawline that could cut glass. Then a woman got out. She looked like she could be a model in a shampoo commercial and could finish a triathlon while simultaneously making scrambled eggs and toast.

The couple held hands for a moment while staring at the house. Then the woman turned back to the car and shouted, "Derek, let's go!"

"Come on, son!" the dad yelled.

And then, out *he* came.

A boy stepped out of the car. Slowly. He was wearing a suit. A *nice* suit. Much shinier and less rumpled (not to mention with fewer holes) than the one I had worn to my aunt Gertrude's wedding. The kid's jet-black hair was parted so severely that it looked like it could hold a piece of paper straight up in the air. I sniffed. My hair was a kind of reddish brown, and no matter how many times I combed it, it always tended to look like I'd just been caught in a hurricane.

His eyes were hidden behind a pair of reflective sunglasses. The boy, Derek, joined his parents. Then suddenly he stopped, flipped off the sunglasses…and looked straight at Kyle and me.

I grabbed Kyle by the jacket and yanked him inside our house. We huddled in the doorway, staring out the window, waiting for this Derek kid to enter 7 Sunnyvale Drive. He joined his parents, walked inside, and when the door closed behind him we finally caught our breath.

"Hey, boys. Oh, hey, Kyle," came my dad's voice. He was sitting at the kitchen table, drinking a cup of coffee while wearing a bathrobe that was open enough to reveal a circular patch of hair around his belly button. "Zeke, don't you have school today?"

"Hey, Mr. Bartholomew," Kyle said. "We were just watching the—"

I elbowed Kyle in the side. He made a meek grunting noise. "We were just watching the grass, and it made me realize that I forgot my social studies homework."

"Good thinking," my dad said, absently scratching his patch of belly button hair. "Have a good day at school. Kyle, make sure Zeke pays attention."

"Will do, Mr. Bartholomew," Kyle said. I debated elbowing him again but decided he'd had enough.

"See you later, kids," Dad said, slurping his coffee, a few drops spilling onto the newspaper.

My dad has taken care of me by himself since my mom died when I was six. He never really talks about her, but I know he misses her. And he never really goes out, just comes home from work, reads or watches TV, and goes to sleep. He makes the best meals on the planet, even though he didn't learn to cook until after my mom was gone. I was young, but I still miss her, miss the few memories I have, and the memories I missed out on. And every now and then I catch my dad leafing through old photo albums, his eyes red, lip trembling. I love him so much. I want to be the best son I can be. Sometimes I wonder if he's proud of me. He always tells me he is, but I'm not any good at baseball, can't run very fast, and my singing voice scares away all the neighborhood cats. Maybe that's why I love reading about spies. Maybe I want to save the world. Let everyone know that Bartholomew kid is just as good as his dad.

I led Kyle up the stairs to my room. I had to keep up appearances that I had actually forgotten my homework. I opened the door to my room.

"What are the chances," Kyle said, "that a spy would move in next to *you?*"

"A million to one," I said.

"More like a *billion* to one. I mean, look at your room, Zeke. Just *look* at it."

Kyle was right. The odds probably were closer to a billion to one.

I'm going to come clean: I love spies. Love everything about them. I love the exciting adventures. The dangerous missions. The exotic locations. The bad guys. The danger. Anyone who enters my room can tell within half a nanosecond.

Plastered all over my walls are posters of dashing rogues and femmes fatales. Piled high on my shelf are DVDs of every spy movie ever made. Underneath that are dozens of books on spies, spy craft, gadgets, and tactics, along with novels packed with adventure and derring-do. Books about men and women sent on incredible journeys to prevent the world from being taken over by rich madmen bent on doing something horrible and devious, often involving a laser death ray or an earth-core drilling mechanism.

I hated being "medium everything." I always wanted to be "great at something." And if I couldn't save the world—or at least get a *B* on my geometry exams—I wanted to lose myself in stories of those who could. I tried to immerse myself in their world, but I don't know karate, I've never rappelled down a cliff side, and I've never sneaked into a heavily guarded fortress.

And now an honest-to-goodness spy lived right next door to me. My dreams were just a single door down. Only I had no idea how soon those dreams would turn into a nightmare.

OF COURSE HE'S IN MY HOMEROOM

Fate.

Fate was laughing at me. Because when I walked into Mr. Statler's homeroom that morning, *he* was sitting there. I don't know how he got to school before me, but I figured he probably owned a motorcycle, or a hovercraft, or a Star Trek–type device that could teleport him from 7 Sunnyvale Drive to Randolph Middle School in itsy-bitsy kid particles.

But there he was. My new neighbor. Derek. And he was sitting next to Donna Okin. I had to stop my jaw from dropping. Kyle was not so tactful.

"Close your mouth, geekwad," I whispered.

"Fneh," said Kyle.

Derek was still wearing his suit, which was complemented by a snazzy royal-blue tie. His hair still looked like it had been parted with a pitchfork, and his sunglasses were tucked into his suit jacket pocket. Donna didn't seem to mind that he was sitting next to her. In fact, she seemed to very much not mind. She was smiling while crooking her neck, trying very, *very* hard to get Derek to notice her neck-crooking.

"I didn't know necks could bend that way," Kyle whispered.

"Pfft," I replied. "No big deal."

But it *was* a big deal. I've gone to school with Donna Okin for nine years, and I've never had the courage to sit next to her. She's never even tried to get my attention, or the attention of any other boy, for that matter. She always sits next to her two best friends, Cynthia Rothstein and Renee Sacks, but always keeps one chair open close by, almost daring anyone to venture into the lion's den. And then *he* walks in, takes that chair, and Donna's neck turns into a Slinky. Okay, I'll admit it. Part of me was jealous that I wasn't sitting next to him. I wanted to ask him a million questions. Where has he traveled? Has he ever fought a super-villain? Has he ever surfed atop a tsunami?

But I was next to Kyle. I *always* sit next to Kyle. Excitement central. Kyle's a great friend and all, but he's about as far from a superspy as I am. Most days Kyle and I sit and goof off, making fun of kids who suck (aka kids who are more popular than us, aka just about everybody). Or we make fun of PB&J.

PB&J is a horrific pop group consisting of two kids, Penny Bowers and Jimmy Peppers, who sing songs so bad that if my ears could cry and wave a white flag, they would. Yet Kyle and I are in the minority. They've sold something like a kajillion albums, played to sold-out arenas, and never seem to break a sweat. Ten minutes of dodgeball and I look like a drowned rat, but these kids' hairstyles are like impenetrable shields made of titanium.

Penny always wears pigtails and more makeup than is appropriate for any twelve-year-old, and Jimmy's sandy blond locks are always shiny and matted down, making it look as though his forehead is trying to peek out through strands of glistening hair. They both sing like they have tubes of sugar hardwired into their bloodstreams, and they suck big time.

I took my customary seat next to Kyle, who whispered, "He's sitting next to Donna Okin." Donna Okin loves PB&J, particularly their new hit song "I Think U R Neat." So does every other girl in the seventh grade at

Randolph. Which means that the smart guys (aka Not Us) pretend to like them too.

"I didn't notice," I said.

"I think she likes him," Kyle said.

"Who cares? He sucks," was my witty reply. Especially because I said it with no conviction whatsoever. "Besides, what does Derek have that I don't?"

"A cool suit. And sunglasses."

"I could get those. I have much more to offer than stupid Derek."

"He also has, like, plutonium luggage."

"Yeah, well, I have cool stuff too."

"That's true," Kyle said. "Like right now, you have gum stuck to your butt."

I whipped around and glared at Kyle. "No, I don't."

"Zeke, I swear. Gum. On your right butt. Cheek. See for yourself."

Sighing, I picked my right butt cheek off the chair ever so slightly and gave it an ultra-quick pat down. I closed my eyes when I felt the sticky residue of gum.

"I told you," Kyle said.

"Great. Now what do I do?"

Kyle shrugged. He stared at Donna looking at Derek.

Long enough to make me nudge him for being such an obvious dolt.

Kyle said, “I bet Derek doesn’t have gum stuck to his butt. I bet there’s a special anti-gum serum on his butt that prevents gum from sticking to it.”

“How could she like him?” I said softly. “They just met. And besides, who wears a suit and tie in the seventh grade?”

Donna Okin was twirling one of her blond curls around her finger and staring at Derek from the corner of her eye. She was eyeing him the same way I eye the stove when my dad makes blueberry pancakes.

Our homeroom teacher, Mr. Statler, came in and closed the door. He took his customary seat on top of his desk. I don’t think I’ve ever seen Mr. Statler use the chair. I think he thinks sitting on the desk makes him look cooler, but all it does is hike up his corduroy pants so we can see his pale ankles.

“Ladies and gentlemen,” Mr. Statler said. He always starts with “ladies and gentlemen,” as though we were attending an opera. “I’d like to introduce a new student who will be joining us here at Randolph. Please welcome our newest addition, Derek Lance.”

Everyone's eyes went to the new kid. Derek Lance. Derek didn't move.

Mr. Statler said, "Derek just moved here from...where did you say you moved from, Derek?"

"I didn't," said Derek.

"I...I'm sorry?" stammered Mr. Statler.

"I didn't say where I was from."

"Oh. Okay. Right, then. Well, would you like to tell the class where—"

"No."

"I...uh...right. Well, moving on. Please tell us something about yourself, then, Derek."

"I don't like people who ask too many questions," Derek said. "They make me angry." I thought I heard Donna Okin gasp. Or it might have been Kyle. Or Mr. Statler. Or me.

"Right, then," Mr. Statler said, nervously pushing his glasses so high up on his nose his eyebrows could see through them. "Let's talk about tomorrow's assembly."

As Mr. Statler spoke, I turned to look at Derek Lance. He was staring straight ahead. He was looking at nothing in particular, but looking really cool doing it. I tapped Kyle on the shoulder.

"I made a new one," I said. "Wanna see?"

Kyle sighed. "You know the phrase 'mad scientist'? I think you're just a 'bad' scientist."

"You laugh now," I said. "Just wait."

"Should I call the fire department now," he said, "or wait until I spontaneously combust?"

"Ha-ha. Look."

"You've been spending way too much time out there in the lab, Zeke. I'm getting worried about you. I like the cave as much as you do, but it's supposed to be fun. It's not supposed to take over your life. Between this and those 'spies' who moved in next door, you're going off the deep end."

"I don't spend too much time there," I said, unconvinced of my own words. "You used to like spending time there with me. You put up as many blueprints as I did. Enjoyed the designs."

"And then I grew up. I don't want to be a loser forever, Zeke. Spending time in that dungeon keeps us frozen in time. I don't want that."

"Suit yourself. I'm happy down there."

"Happy? Or delusional, Mr. Bond?"

I ignored this comment.

For years, I've been an amateur inventor. Kyle has

witnessed most of my crafts firsthand—and has had many, many eyebrows and armhairs singed off due to my more juvenile efforts.

The first gadget he ever saw me make was an infrared motion detector that I assembled using a laser pointer, a couple of nine-volt batteries, and the reflector from my bike. I mounted it at the foot of the stairs to my room so that my dad would trip it whenever he was coming upstairs. That way I'd have plenty of time to turn off any computer games and pick up a math book before he opened the door. The problem was that the device was *way* too sensitive. It picked up my dad, discarded shoes, even large particles of dust. The first time I tried the device, the alarm went off so often that I developed a nervous tic. Still, I knew I had talent and vision. Parts are another story. Twice our local neighborhood watch has been told to keep an eye out for a "curly-haired man, possibly a midget or leprechaun, looting trash cans." I mean I'm not as tall as Kyle, but I'm *definitely* not a midget.

"So check this out," I said, reaching into my blue backpack. Kyle looked a little skeptical when I pulled out a peanut butter and jelly sandwich.

"I think that's already been invented," he said.

"No, that's my test subject," I replied. Then I showed him a small device about the size of a pencil sharpener with a digital watch face mounted on top.

"I didn't bring safety goggles," he said. "What is that thing? Is it dangerous?"

"It's a peanut butter and jelly sandwich," I said.

"Is that a tribute to Penny Bowers and Jimmy Peppers?"

"What? Of course not."

"You mean you're not excited for the debut of their new video tomorrow? The whole world is gonna see it. And we're gonna be a *part* of that world!"

"I'd rather poke out my eyeballs with a rubber duck than watch the new PB&J video," I said.

"Well, you're the only one who doesn't care," Kyle said. "I hate them too, but I want to be able to come in to school and be able to talk about it."

"Pfft. Whatever."

"So what is that gizmo anyway?" Kyle asked.

"Oh, right. It's an automatic sandwich-crust slicer. Easy to make. Just a Sabertronics pager motor, a piece of a box-cutter blade, a few nuts and bolts, a calculator watch, and a triple-A battery. Watch." Kyle winced when I pressed a button on the gizmo, turned a few dials, then placed it on top of the sandwich. "You simply enter the dimensions of your sandwich, and it automatically cuts the edges off to your exact specifications."

"Wow. I don't know how I've lived so long without one of those," he said.

"You laugh now, but this machine will save you precious sandwich-crust slicing time. Behold."

I pressed the Enter button on the watch. The device made a soft *snick* sound. "That's the retractable blade," I told Kyle. "It doesn't descend until you press Enter."

"Or until it gets jostled in your pocket and stabs you in the thigh."

"You're so cynical," I said. "Just watch."

I placed the device at the edge of the sandwich, keyed in the sandwich dimension, and pressed Enter again. Suddenly the machine began to whir—way too loud. It began to saw its way around the sandwich, making an awful *scree scree* noise as it did. Even Mr. Statler noticed. Then Isabel Berg, a freckled, pigtailed girl and the quietest kid in our homeroom, clapped her hands to her head and began to scream like her ears were on fire. And when Isabel Berg made any kind of sound, something was definitely wrong.

When the device was finished cutting the sandwich, it stopped. It had cut a perfect square around the sandwich edges. I looked at Kyle triumphantly.

"See, I told you it…"

At that moment the sandwich disappeared, falling through a sandwich-sized hole the device had cut through the desk itself. I felt my face grow hot. Kyle and I peered through the square hole in my desk to see the sandwich resting peacefully on the classroom floor.

The classroom went quiet, except for one voice.

"This is Stefan Holt, reporting live from the scene."

I groaned. Stefan Holt sat three chairs over from me. He had sandy blond hair and always wore a long dress shirt with the sleeves rolled up. Every time something out of the ordinary occurred, he acted like he was some kind of television reporter, holding a pen to his mouth like he was speaking into a microphone and being broadcast all over the world. Funny when it was about someone else. Not so funny when he was "reporting" about you.

"There appears to be an equipment malfunction in the homeroom class of Mr. Reginald Statler. The perpetrator, one Ezekiel Bartholomew, could not be reached for comment."

"You didn't even ask me," I said.

"Video of Mr. Bartholomew shows the young mad genius red in the face at his latest debacle. Reactions are pouring in from around the globe, and most are appalled at this lack of civility."

"Lack of what?" I said.

"There are rumors, unfounded so far, that Mr. Bartholomew has also peed his pants."

A healthy laugh went up from the kids in the room. Mr. Statler tried to calm them down, but couldn't be heard over the roaring. If my face wasn't red before, it was probably a deep purple now.

Finally the room quieted down. Stefan Holt had put his pen back in his desk. Guess the cameras had turned off.

Then I heard a quiet, cocky laugh. I looked up to see the smiling face of Derek Lance. He was staring right at me. Waiting until his mocking could be heard. It was a belly laugh, almost like he was trying too hard, but there was something beneath it, as though his mocking was personal in a weird way.

"Mr. Bartholomew?" Mr. Statler said.

"I know, I know," I sighed. "See you in detention."

Mr. Statler nodded. "And no more of your gizmos in homeroom, otherwise I'll see you in detention every day for a month."

Derek Lance had stopped snickering, but the cocky smile remained on his face. It was imperceptible to anyone else, I think, but he shook his head slightly. Disdainfully. The head shake said one thing: *amateur.*

For some reason, this mocking cut me deeper than Donna Okin, the laughter, or Stefan Holt. There was something about Derek Lance that made me uncomfortable. Like he knew who I was, knew what I was trying to do, and was able to cut just in the right spot to strike a nerve. And he had.

"You know," Kyle said, "I bet that gadget has at least one thing going for it."

"Oh, really? What?"

"We could use it to cut the gum off your butt."

"You know I hate you, right?"

"Don't blame the peanut gallery."

I ignored Kyle and gritted my teeth. I knew right then and there that I had to turn the tables. I had to know just who Derek Lance was. I had to spy on the spy.

GETTING MY HANDS (AND EVERYTHING ELSE) DIRTY

That night I did what any self-respecting adventurous spy would do—I went through Derek Lance's trash cans.

I waited until after my stomach was bursting with a double helping of my dad's famous spaghetti and meatballs and he was crashed on the couch watching *Law & Order* reruns. Then I slipped on a pair of navy blue sweatpants and a gray hooded sweatshirt (I didn't own black). I tried on a pair of cheapo sunglasses, but took them off after I bumped into a tree outside.

Using the cloak of darkness—or, more accurately, simply hoping nobody saw me—I crept into the Lances' front yard. Two trash bins were sitting on the curb, filled with all sorts of junk.

Quietly I removed the lids from the trash bins,

took a pen from my pocket, and began to dig through their garbage.

The top layer was your common junk pile. Soda cans, packing peanuts, empty microwave food boxes. Apparently Derek and I had one thing in common: we both liked fish sticks. Below the fish stick boxes I found the first clue: discarded maps from all over the world. Honduras. The Netherlands. Prague. Iceland. Costa Rica. Beijing. No doubt souvenirs from Derek Lance's travels around the globe.

Under the maps I found something even more interesting.

A compass with a cracked face. It looked heavily used and didn't appear to be working. Below that I came upon something even more curious: a small blue pillbox with one word printed on the side: IPECAC.

Whoa. Syrup of ipecac was something spies commonly used when they were poisoned. It was derived from the ipecacuanha plant and, when synthesized, was used to induce vomiting. If a spy was poisoned, a dollop of ipecac syrup would help him upchuck any evil goop he'd been forced to drink. I'd never heard of it existing in pill form. That sounded like some heavy-duty spy stuff, formulated in some underground lab where bespectacled scientists spent hours figuring out how best to make secret agents puke. Awesome.

I popped the pillbox in my pocket and continued searching. Soon I found a pair of sunglasses…just like the ones Derek Lance wore.

I wiped them off, placed them over my eyes, and practiced my best spy impersonation.

"Hey, I'm Derek Lance," I said to nobody in particular. "Freeze. I'm Derek Lance. Agent Lance. That's me, all right. You have the right to remain awesome."

I cringed. Wow. I made an even dorkier spy than I thought. Still, if I had access to the kind of technology and equipment that Derek Lance did, I'd be able to create some of the coolest devices ever known. Either way, I decided to keep the shades.

Then, below a few billion packing peanuts, I found a cardboard box for something called a "Red-i-Cam." The box had contained a small, mountable surveillance camera. I dug deeper and found five more empty Red-i-Cam boxes. I turned around, looked up. And saw them.

One Red-i-Cam was bolted to the Lances' front door, right above the peephole. Several others were mounted over the windows. Another hung over the garage. Clearly the Lance family wanted to know about everything and everyone who came near their house.

My blood ran cold. They could probably see me at this very moment. And in my dark sweatpants and sweatshirt, wearing a pair of aviator sunglasses, I probably looked like a short, nervous burglar. Nice going, Zeke.

Hastily I put the lids back on the trash cans and turned to head home. Just as I fastened the last lid on, however, a car pulled up in the Lances' driveway and I was frozen between a pair of ultra-bright headlights.

This was really not good…

The car was sleek and black and the windows were tinted. I didn't know what to do. If I ran, they'd know I was up to something. And if I stayed put, they'd still know I was up to something. So I did what I always do when I get nervous—I got the hiccups. As I held my breath, the passenger door opened.

The engine was still running when out stepped a man wearing a dark suit and sunglasses. He walked around to where I stood, never taking his gaze from me. I tried to think of a million things to say, some sort of excuse as to why I was there.

The man walked up to me, stopped, and to my surprise said, "Agent Derek Lance?"

Agent Derek Lance. I was right. Derek Lance *was* a spy!

I could have replied any way I wanted, and to this day I don't know why I said what I did. I responded with six simple words: "Yes, I am agent Derek Lance."

The man nodded and mumbled something into a microphone attached to his sleeve that sounded like "Mr. Safari." Then he said, "Come with us."

The agent opened the back door of the sedan. Another agent was sitting there, along with a driver, both wearing the same suit getup. The man in the backseat nodded. "It's an honor to meet you, Agent Lance."

"Likewise," I said, slipping in next to him. I know you're never supposed to get in cars with strangers, but something about this felt right. My whole life I'd wanted to be a spy, and even if I couldn't be Derek Lance, I could at least feel what it was like to be him for one night before they discovered I was lame old Ezekiel Bartholomew. "Medium everything."

The car pulled away from the Lance home. The three agents stayed silent. After about ten minutes, I said, "So...where to?"

The men laughed. "You know where we're headed, Agent Lance. He's dying to meet you."

"Oh, I'm looking forward to meeting, um, *him* too," I said stupidly. "Just forgot the address is all."

"Understandable. He doesn't like people to remember where his headquarters is located."

"Right. Well…he's done a very good job keeping it hidden."

"He works quite hard to maintain secrecy," the man next to me said.

"*Quite* hard," the driver seconded.

"Extremely hard," the third man said.

"He works hard. Got it," I said.

"Before we arrive at our destination," the man next to me said, "we need to be certain that you have the codes."

My eyes went wide.

"The…codes?"

"Yes. As you know, Operation Songbird is scheduled to go into effect in twenty-four hours. SirEebro cannot be activated without the codes. That is why you're here."

"Of course, SirEebro and Operation Songbird," I said, playing it off. "But, you know, I'd rather wait until we get there before I give them to you. If that's okay." I figured that would at least buy me some time to figure out what to do.

One of the agents up front spoke into a microphone. I only made out *codes...wants to wait...affirmative.*

The man turned back to face me. "Mr. Le Carré understands your concerns. However, he requires you to reveal one of the three codes right now. The others can wait until we arrive, as you desire."

"Right. One code. Out of three. No problem." I thought about all the spy books and movies I'd memorized. They always spoke in code. I remembered enough to give it a shot. "Alpha. Tango. Bravo..."

The man next to me screwed up his lip.

"Is this a joke?" he said.

"Um...no. No joke," I said. I was getting nervous. Being Derek Lance wasn't what I'd expected.

"Don't play stupid with us, Agent Lance."

"I'm not playing," I said.

"We all know that the codes for SirEebro are numeric."

The codes for SirEebro were numeric. Of course they were.

"Agent Lance," one of the men in front said angrily, "what are you trying to pull?"

"Is it about the money?" the man next to me said. "You're being compensated quite handsomely for Operation Songbird."

Okay, it was time to end this charade. I didn't know what Agent Derek Lance was involved in, but it didn't seem like it would be too good for my Zeke Bartholomew.

"It's not the money," I said. "It's just that I don't have the codes."

"Agent Lance, we are *not* playing a game," one of the men said, anger rising in his voice. "If you are unable to give us the codes, you are worthless to Mr. Le Carré. And since you know what the codes are being used for, since you know about Operation Songbird, and since so much and so many lives are at stake, if you cannot give us the codes, we cannot let you leave."

"If you can't give us the codes for SirEebro," the agent next to me said coldly, "we have no choice but to kill you."

My heart hammered in my chest. I didn't know what to do or what to say. *Kill me? Lives at stake?* Even if they believed I wasn't Derek Lance, they'd already said too much. They wouldn't let me live. Suddenly, playing Derek Lance wasn't so much fun anymore. Suddenly, being a spy wasn't such a glamorous idea.

"What if I weren't Agent Lance?" I said nervously. The driver laughed.

"Right. We just happened to pick up a random kid standing in front of Derek Lance's house. Besides, I'd recognize those sunglasses anywhere, Agent Lance."

Those stupid sunglasses! This didn't sit too well. In fact, it *really* didn't sit too well with my stomach. Then I remembered. *The ipecac.*

"I think I'm going to be sick," I moaned.

"Enough games, Agent Lance," the agent next to me said. "We're not in the mood..."

I leaned forward, pretended to cough, and quickly slipped the ipecac pill into my mouth. It lodged in my throat. Of course it did.

"Do you have any water? Bit of a scratchy throat."

The agent next to me handed me a bottle of water. I drank it and felt the pill slip down into my belly. I smiled. It worked.

Then my smile vanished. Within five seconds my stomach felt like it was rolling and pitching on the high seas. And this storm wasn't about to end well.

"Oh, no," I whimpered. "Spaghetti and meatballs..."

Suddenly I lurched forward and puked up my

spaghetti-and-meatball dinner all over the driver. He shrieked and lost control of the wheel. The sedan skidded across the road, the tires making an awful rubbery screech. I upchucked all over the three agents, who screamed and tried to dodge the mess. No such luck. I'd had a big dinner.

Then I felt a huge jolt as the car slammed into something. Sparks flew up around us. My teeth rattled, and my shoulder slammed into the door hard, sending pain searing through my body. The seat belt kept me from being thrown into the windshield. Then we were spinning, around and around and around. If I hadn't already puked, this spin cycle would have done it for sure.

The four of us held on for dear life as the car rotated again and again, finally coming to a stop after about ten spins. I opened my eyes. The car was a complete mess. The agents were groggy, preoccupied with the grossness. This was my only chance.

I unbuckled my seat belt, threw open the door, and ran out into the night. The car had stopped on the middle of a bridge, diagonally cutting across two lanes. I was fifty yards away from either end of the bridge. No-man's-land.

Then I heard someone yell, "Freeze, Agent Lance! Move and you're dead."

I slowly turned around. The driver was standing there, nasty spaghetti strands dangling from his sunglasses. I felt a burp rise in my chest.

"I knew you were dangerous, Agent Lance," he said, "but we clearly underestimated your diversionary skills. Now get back in the car and give us the codes."

I started to walk backward. I couldn't get back in the car, but I didn't have time to run. The muzzle was pointed right at me. "I can't!" I shouted.

"You can and you will. Right now, or you're one dead spy."

I kept backing up, kept telling myself, *This isn't happening. This isn't happening.* Then the armed agent held out his hand and stepped forward. "Be careful, Agent Lance!" he shouted.

Just then I felt the guardrail clip my knees from behind. And as I toppled over the guardrail into the abyss below, I heard my own voice echoing in the night: "*I'm not Derek Lance!*"

THE PEN IS MIGHTIER THAN...NEVER MIND

The first time I tried to swim on my own I was five years old. The town swimming pool was free to anyone who registered with city hall, and as soon as my arms fit into floaties my mom dragged me over and carried me into the water. My mom would always wear a one-piece with some sort of floral design. My dad wore swim trunks and a T-shirt. He never took off his shirt. He's kind of pale guy, so I think he might have been worried that if he took off his shirt on a sunny day he might spontaneously burst into flame.

So one day, when my parents weren't looking, I ran and dove into the pool to show them that I didn't need those stupid floaties. I was a big boy and didn't need their eyes on me at all times.

I did my best cannonball and splashed down in the

deep end hard enough to drive the air from my lungs. Fifteen seconds passed. Thirty. Forty-five. I was doing it. I was swimming alone. Then suddenly I realized that in all of my excitement, I'd forgotten to breathe.

And that's when I felt a pair of hands grab me around my waist and hoist me out of the water, sputtering like a perforated garden hose. It was my dad. He was holding me and crying. And he still had his shirt on.

"What in the heck did you think you were doing?" he shouted, the fear in his eyes far greater than any anger.

I shrugged and said, "Proving to you and Mom I could do it. Swim alone."

He hugged me tight and said, "I'll never doubt that you can do anything, Zeke."

My dad hoisted me out of the pool and plopped me on the ground. And that's when I realized that, in my hasty dive, somehow my pants has come off. I stood there butt naked for about ten seconds before my father realized what had happened. My bathing suit was floating on the surface like an unmanned vessel. He plucked it out, picked me up, and carried me into the bathroom. So much for feeling like an adult.

That years-old memory ran through my head when I

realized, once again, that I'd forgotten to breathe.

I lurched out of the water, my eyes, nose, and brain burning. Where was I? What had happened? Then I remembered the suited man pointing the gun at me. I remembered backing up, holding my hands out, and then...darkness.

Wiping the water from my eyes, I looked around. Everything was dark. I couldn't make out much of anything. Thankfully I'd become a much better swimmer since that day at the pool, so I was able to tread water while figuring out just what to do.

The current was fairly strong. My sweatpants were waterlogged and heavy, and they were dragging me down. I couldn't see a riverbank, so I began to paddle in a random direction hoping to strike land.

Bad idea, Zeke.

About a dozen strokes in, a massive light appeared above me, shining directly into the path I was swimming toward. The light flooded my eyes, blinding me. It was coming from the bridge I'd just fallen off. The goons were looking for me.

Yesterday I had been in math class. Ms. Connelly was glaring at me because I wasn't paying attention and didn't hear her ask me a question. I thought I was in big trouble then. I didn't know what big trouble was.

When my vision adjusted to the darkness, I could see that the goons were climbing down the riverbank to try to spot me from there. I could hold my breath for a minute—two, tops—but these guys were pros.

Advantage goons.

The light drew closer. The goons would spot me in a matter of seconds. Then I heard a voice, and my heart froze in my chest.

"Lance has to be here somewhere." It was the goon who had sat next to me in the car. "Kid fell straight down. I heard a splash. He's in the water."

"Ugh, I have spaghetti strands in my hair," another goon said.

"He's smarter than we thought," the first voice said. "Obviously Derek Lance has the ability to innately control his gag reflex. Mr. Le Carré should have warned us about who we were going up against."

"He's still a kid, and there are three of us. All we gotta do is find him."

"I owe Lance a broken leg. Maybe two. Ugh, I think there's meatball in my nostril."

I'd thrown up dozens of times in my life, and never once had it been considered "resourceful." But that awkward sense of pride died down when I remembered that these goons still thought I was Derek Lance, and just a moment ago they'd threatened to kill me. I decided it wasn't the best course of action to wait around for them to find me.

The problem was I didn't know where to go. If I made any noise they might hear me, and I didn't know how far the other riverbank was.

Through the dim light I could see steel supports rising from the water like rusty gray sentries. A bed of reeds and lily pads swayed underneath the bridge. And that's when I got the idea that I thought might just save my life.

I dug into my pocket and found the pen I'd used to sift through Derek Lance's trash. At first I wondered if I could throw it at one of the lackeys, maybe do some sort of boomerang thing where it knocked all three of them out cold. Then I remembered that I have the arm strength of a wet noodle. Maybe I could write a note on a leaf, stick it inside a bottle. Yeah, right.

I uncapped the pen. I must not have been paying attention, because I felt the cartridge crack. That's when the idea came to me. Maybe I wasn't as stupid as I thought I was…

I worked the barrel of the pen back and forth until the cartridge split in two. I let the closed-off end float away and brought the other end to my lips. I blew as hard as I could. A nasty, inky taste flooded my mouth. Blech. This had better work…

I dove below the surface and quietly swam over to the reed bed, wary of creating too much attention and drawing the goons to my position. Once I was nestled in with the reeds, I pinched the ink tube, pulled it out, and let it drift away. Then I brought the newly created breathing tube to my mouth, ducked underwater, and hovered just below the surface with the tip of my new breathing straw poking just above the waterline.

Then I waited.

I couldn't draw much air through the tube, and I had to tread water just below the surface to keep the tube out of the water. I wouldn't be able to do this for very long. My arm muscles were growing stiff from treading water, but my life depended on it.

Just then, I saw a wave of light sweep across the water directly above where I was hiding. Then another.

Then another. My eyes widened, water stinging them. Each of the three goons was scanning the river with a flashlight. I was scared to breathe, scared to move. What if the breathing tube dipped underwater for a moment and I accidentally blew bubbles? Not only would I get caught, but I'd die with inky blue lips. Real heroic.

Hold it together, Zeke...

I heard noises above the surface, but couldn't make them out. The men were clearly shouting. Frustrated at something. The flashlights had come to rest directly above my hiding spot. I breathed in and out as slowly as I possibly could. The pen tube was incredibly slim and still tasted kind of nasty. I only had a few more seconds before my arms would cramp up.

Then the lights were gone. The shouting was growing distant. I peeked my eyes above the surface. The goons were walking back up the riverbank toward the car. They were leaving.

"Mr. Le Carré is going to be pretty peeved," one of the goons said.

"*You* were in the backseat with him. He's a freakin' kid, and you couldn't restrain him?"

"Lay off; there's a reason Mr. Le Carré sent three of us. This isn't an ordinary kid."

"We know that now," the driver said. "We only have one choice."

"No…him? You're going to call *him?*"

The goon said the word *him* like "him" was the last person you'd ever want to meet in a dark alley.

"We can't. He can kill Lance with his pinky finger."

They were too far away. I couldn't make out what the driver was saying. All I heard was something that sounded like, "*Call hag rock.*"

I didn't know what a "hag rock" was, and even though it sounded silly, if it was bad enough to have these goons quaking in their penny loafers, it was bad enough to make me want to get the heck away from it.

I waited until the car had driven away, then slowly swam to the riverbank, launched myself onto the muddy grass, and breathed in deep, thankful gulps of air. I sat there in the mud and gloom for what must have been an hour. I wanted to make sure the goons were gone—and that they weren't coming back. Every so often I would hear the roar of traffic, the honking of horns, see glimpses of headlights. And each time, I hunkered down, ready to dive back into the murky depths should the goon squad realize I had been able to shake them.

When I was reasonably certain they were gone, I stood up. I shivered. The night air was cool, but my soaked clothes only made it worse. I took off my shirt and wrung it out. Then I took off my pants. They were caked in grass and leaves and grime. I washed them off in the river, then tied them around my waist. They would dry while I walked.

The whole night seemed surreal. Just a short while ago I had been twirling spaghetti around my fork, ready to hunker down and study ancient Rome, and now here I was, rolling around in the dirt, evading a bunch of evil dudes who may or may not be serious in doing me bodily harm.

I had no idea where I was. We had been driving for between thirty and forty minutes before the, um, spaghetti incident. My best guess was that I was between twenty and thirty miles away from home. I didn't have a phone on me, or any money or identification. All I had were my wits.

Which meant I was kind of screwed.

Come on, Zeke, I thought. *You're not as dumb as you think.*

Okay. I used to love reading about constellations. Stars and their alignment in the sky. I used to peruse maps of the sky, dreaming of becoming Sagittarius, the Archer, and doing battle with the Hydra, the deadly Water Serpent.

I looked up, trying to use the map of the sky to determine where I was. I scanned the thousands of tiny specks, looking for a clue, something that would allow me to gain my bearing.

Then I saw it. Auriga, the Charioteer. At ten times the size of the sun, Auriga is one of the brighter constellations. I couldn't miss it for the world.

Then, slightly above and to the right of Auriga was Perseus, named after one of Zeus's children (it also happened to be the name of a character in one of my favorite series of books). In the sky, Perseus was slightly northeast of Auriga. I was getting somewhere. I was gaining my bearings.

I began to think I was kind of a bright kid, despite what my teachers said.

Farther past Perseus was Triangulum, the Triangle; Andromeda; and Lacerta, the Lizard. Using those bearings, I knew I had to head eastward. To follow those stars.

I wasn't sure if I could walk the full twenty-plus miles to my home in the middle of the night, freezing my butt off, but at least I'd be heading in the right direction.

I climbed up the riverbank, gripping trees and finding footholds among the mud. By the time I got to the bridge I was a sopping, cold, dirty mess, like a pale swamp monster that had just climbed out of the murk in desperate need of a suntan. I began to walk down the road.

My knees were shaking. From time to time cars would pass—but none of them stopped. I held my thumb out like I'd seen in so many movies, but let's be honest. If I saw a dirty kid asking for a ride by the side of the road, I'd probably think he was some sort of hermit waiting to steal my car and then all of my gold.

I kept my mind occupied by replaying some of my favorite spy movies in my head. I wondered what James Bond would do in my situation. I laughed to myself. Bond would have never found himself in this situation. He would have beaten the goons to a pulp, made them compliment his natty suit and impeccable hair, then had a torrid affair with a beautiful bikini model who also happened to be a nuclear physicist.

But I wasn't James Bond. I wasn't a cool kid spy like

Alex Rider. I wasn't a spy. I was a twelve-year-old kid with bad hair and occasional acne outbreaks.

Eventually there were no more cars on the road. The moon hung high in the night sky like a brilliant orb. The wind chill grew worse. My teeth were chattering. My hands were shaking. My bones felt tired. I wasn't sure how much longer I could walk.

Then, up in the distance, I saw a warm glow. It was a house, with the downstairs lights on. My eyes grew wide. Somebody was home. Somebody could help me. Surely they'd have a phone I could use, a glass of water to hydrate my aching muscles.

I trudged toward the house, my efforts redoubled. In just a few short steps I would be greeted by an energetic family with warm blankets and soup and a dog to sleep at my feet.

Okay, I could still dream despite everything.

I braced myself on the railing and heaved myself up the front steps. It was an old house with wood that smelled faintly of mildew. A porch swing creaked gently in the wind, its moldy seat and rusty chains looking like its last inhabitants had lived there sometime around the time the last of the dinosaurs died off. The house would have looked desolate and deserted (not to mention really creepy) if the lights hadn't been on.

I knocked on the door, then resumed rubbing my hands together either in the hopes of staying warm or somehow miraculously starting a fire. I waited a few minutes. Nobody answered.

I peeked in the window. I couldn't see anyone, but there was a light orange couch and a throw rug and some other furniture and decorations. A mug rested on a glass coffee table, thin wisps of smoke wafting from its lip. Somebody was drinking coffee or tea. Somebody was home.

I knocked again. Harder this time.

"Just a minute!" a female voice said from inside. I took a step back and put on my best pouty face to make her feel bad for me. A moment later the door opened. Standing there was an old woman, likely in her late seventies or eighties—or maybe nineties. I think at some point it's hard to tell the difference.

She was wearing a dark brown shawl, and her gray hair cascaded around her face in smoky ringlets. Her arms and hands were dotted with liver spots. When she saw me, her eyes widened and she beckoned me to step inside.

"Oh, my goodness, child! What on earth are you

doing here in the middle of nowhere at such an ungodly hour? And why are you so filthy?" She squinted her eyes slightly. "And why aren't you wearing any pants?"

I looked down and immediately felt my face flush. I'd completely forgotten that I'd tied my now-crusty sweatpants around my waist.

"I…I'm sorry. I fell into the river and—"

"Say no more." She hustled over to a closet and swung it open. She rummaged around and came out with a pair of trousers. "Here. The bathroom is down the hall. Put these on. I'll start a kettle."

I followed her directions and went to the bathroom. It was full of ornately decorated soaps and candles, and the bathtub was one of those old-fashioned types that rested on porcelain feet. I stripped off my nasty sweatpants, hung them on the shower rod, and pulled on the beige trousers. They were a little stiff and a little too roomy, but they were clean and that's all that mattered.

I washed my face and hands with a bar of soap, then wrung myself dry, afraid to dirty one of the clean towels. When I was finished I stepped out. The woman was waiting for me with a hot mug. She handed it to me.

"Chamomile, with a touch of lemon and honey."

"Thank you," I said. "My name is Zeke. You have a beautiful home."

"Gertie Zimmerman," the woman said. "And you don't have to lie about my home."

"I'm not lying. It's very nice."

"Oh, stop. It smells like old people and marmalade."

"I was going to say freshly cut grass covered in cheddar cheese, but I see where you're coming from."

"I can't stand this place," Gertie sighed, pressing the back of her hand to her forehead in a dramatic gesture that signified either exhaustion or worry that her brain might leak out through her head pores. "But I'm too old to move and don't have the money to buy anything better. Sometimes I wish the Lord would just burn it to the ground so I could collect the insurance and move elsewhere."

Come to think of it, the house did smell a bit like marmalade. And I was reasonably sure there was no actual marmalade in the house. I shuddered thinking of what the smell might actually be.

"Thanks again, Gertie. I'm lost. I was kidnapped—okay, not really kidnapped. Just, um, taken where I didn't want to go. See, I wanted to go with them at first, but then there were codes and goons and spaghetti and—"

"Sounds like you've had quite an adventure. Sit down. Get comfortable." She waved me over to a plush sofa. I sat down gingerly, knowing I wasn't fully clean.

"Thank you for the pants," I said. "Your husband won't mind?"

"Oh, Howard has been dead for twenty years. This is him."

Gertie picked up a photograph and held it out. It was a handsome man with a big, bushy mustache. "My dear Howard Zimmerman. I miss combing his mustache every day of the week."

"Wait…you're saying I'm wearing…your dead husband's pants?"

"Oh, yes. Howard refused to get rid of anything while he was alive, and our son, Harron, refused to take them. Howard always said that as long as there was room in the closet, why waste good clothes? It seemed silly to go against his wishes after he passed on. And now they've come in handy, haven't they, Zeke?"

"Howard didn't…um…die in *these* pants, did he?"

Gertie laughed so hard she held her sides. "Oh, heavens, no! Those particular pants are still hanging in the closet. Would you prefer them? They're corduroy. Nice and warm."

"Um, that's really okay. These are just fine. Gertie, would you mind if I use your phone? I need to call my dad and the police."

"Absolutely. It's right over there."

Gertie pointed at an antique rotary phone hanging on the wall. I picked up the receiver, grimacing when I thought of Howard possibly holding it at some point while wearing these pants. It took a few tries to figure out how to dial, but I finally got through to 911.

"Nine-one-one, what's your emergency?"

"Hi, yeah, my name is Zeke Bartholomew and some guys just tried to kill me."

"Okay, calm down, Zeke."

"I am calm."

"Sir, I'm going to have to ask you to remain calm."

"I am calm. Please, just listen."

"Sir, if this is not a real emergency, I'm going to have to report you."

"Whatever, please report me and then come get me. Look, three goons in suits tried to kill me. They're working for some guy, and I think they're planning something terrible."

"Sir, would you like to report the threat of a terrorist attack?"

"Uh, I don't know what it is. But it's bad. They wouldn't tell me. They thought I was someone else."

"You lied about your identity?"

"Well, um, technically yes, but why should that matter? They tried to kill me!"

"Sir, I'm going to have to ask you to calm down."

"I am calm!"

"Sir, I'm going to report you to our supervisors. Where are you located?"

"Hold on. Gertie, what's the address here?"

"Forty-two Mulberry Lane in Thistlehaven," she replied. "Everything all right, Zack?

"It's Zeke," I said to Gertie, and then to the 911 operator I repeated,"Forty-two Mulberry Lane in Thistlehaven. Hurry. They're looking for me right now."

"And you said your name was Zack?"

"Zeke."

"As in Ezekiel?"

"Does it matter? Zeke Bartholomew. Forty-two Mulberry Lane."

"It says here that Forty-Two Mulberry Lane is registered to a Mr. and Mrs. Howard Zimmerman. Is Mr. Zimmerman there?"

"No, he's dead."

"Are you calling to report a murder?"

"No! No murders! Not yet, though, but if you keep me on the line, that might change if those goons show up."

"Sir, please calm down."

"I don't think you're very good at your job."

"Don't take that tone of voice with me. We'll be sending a car right away, Mr. Berthieume."

"Right. Whatever. Send it quick."

"Good-bye, Mr. Berthieume."

The operator hung up. It took all my willpower not to rip the phone out of the wall and stomp on it. I took a deep breath. But it was Gertie's phone. Besides, I had one more call to make.

I dialed the number. He picked up on the first ring.

"Hello?"

"Dad. It's me."

"Oh, thank god, Zeke. Are you all right? I've been calling everybody."

"I'm okay, Dad. I'm safe. I'm in Thistlehaven."

"Thistlehaven? How did you end up all the way out there?"

"It's a long story. Listen, Dad, the cops are on their way."

"Cops? Zeke, what happened?"

"Please, just listen, Dad. If anyone calls or comes to the door, if you don't recognize them, don't let them in. Especially if they're wearing nice suits."

"Zeke, you're scaring me. Let me come and pick you up. What's your address?"

"I'm at Forty-Two Mulberry Lane. Okay?"

There was no response.

"Hello? Dad?"

There was nobody on the other end. The phone had gone dead.

I put the receiver down and picked it back up. There was no dial tone. My heart began to race.

"Gertie? The phone just went dead."

"Is it plugged in?"

I checked the cord. Yup. All plugged in.

"That's odd," she said. She took the phone from me and held it to her ear. "That's never happened before."

"Did you pay your phone bill?"

"Of course. All my billing is done online through autopay."

I decided against asking Gertie how someone her age knew how to set up autopay considering my dad couldn't even figure out how to set his TiVo, but there was a more pressing issue. Had my dad heard me? He knew I was in Thistlehaven, but it's a pretty big town, and he'd never find me going house to house. Everything was way, way too quiet.

"Just relax," Gertie said. "Sit down. Drink your tea."

I sipped the tea. It tasted like bathwater.

"There, now. Doesn't that help?"

"No," I said. "There's a band of goons out to kill me because they think I have some stupid secret codes. Sorry if your Earl Grey doesn't soothe that."

"Loons? There are loons out to get you? Aren't they extinct?"

"GOONS," I shouted. "Ugh, never mind. Do you have a cell phone?"

"No. Those things will microwave your brain."

"Yeah, well, if the microwave had a way to get in touch with my dad or the cops..."

"I do have my laptop. Grandkids got it for me for my birthday. Darned if I use it for anything other than solitaire."

"A laptop? Where is it?"

"Here. I'll show you."

Gertie led me up a rickety flight of stairs to a guest

room. It was swathed in beige fabrics, and the air was so stale I could probably levitate on it. There was a fairly new Apple laptop sitting on an antique makeup table and plugged into the wall.

"This is perfect. Thanks, Gertie."

I pushed the power button on the laptop and it began to boot up. I figured even if the phones didn't work, I could email my dad with the address.

Then, just as the friendly little Apple logo appeared on the screen, a massive reverberation shook the house. Every light went out. And the computer went dead.

"What…what was that?" Gertie asked, her voice disembodied in the dark.

"Oh…that's not good," I whispered. The reverberation. I knew what it was. The same thing had happened in a spy movie I'd seen. The good spy was infiltrating the enemy camp, and set off something called an EMP. EMP stood for electromagnetic pulse. The EMP was a burst of radiation that caused a fluctuating electric and magnetic field, damaging or simply knocking out any circuitry within a given area. When the spy set off the EMP pulse, it blew out any and all communications devices and sent a barely perceptible surge through the enemy camp.

I know it was just a movie…but I could swear this felt exactly like that.

First the phone dying. Now all the electronic devices were dead. The laptop ran on a battery, so even if there was a downed power line the battery should have still powered it. But, no—the battery was dead.

We were in the dark. Cut off. And I was pretty sure we weren't alone.

"I need to get out of here," I said, bolting up from the table.

Slivers of light streamed in through the windows, allowing just enough light to illuminate the stairway. I cautiously made my way down, Gertie following me.

"What…where are you going, Zeke?"

"They found me," I said, slowly walking through the foyer toward the barely visible front door. I squinted. It was a silhouette in the darkness. My heart hammered. I was sweating through Gertie's dead husband's pants. The only way I could have possibly felt ickier is if I were wearing Gertie's dead husband's underwear under his pants.

"Where are you going to go?" Gertie said, concerned. "It's pitch black outside."

"The longer I stay here, the more trouble you're in."

I should have felt brave saying that. After all, I was offering to leave Gertie's house to protect her. Naturally she would beg me to stay, but I would heroically shrug off her offer and march out into the darkness, alone and unafraid.

"Okay, then. Try not to get lost."

"Wait, that…that's it? You don't want me to stay?"

"Why in the blue heavens would I want that?" Gertie asked. "If you're telling the truth, and loons are after you, why would I want them near my bedroom? So get on with you. But do let me know that you got home safely."

"Yeah. Right. Thanks, Gertie. I'll be sure to call first thing." I wasn't very good at sarcasm, but I felt I had laid it on nice and thick.

I clutched the front door knob and looked back to see if Gertie had changed her mind. It might have been the darkness, but she just stood there.

"Whatcha waiting for? Doors don't open themselves."

"Bye, Gertie."

I turned the door knob…and suddenly an explosion threw me backward. My body slammed against a wall, and I crumpled to the floor, dazed.

"What the heck…" I muttered, slowly getting to my

knees. I looked up. And after how I reacted to what I saw standing in the decimated doorway, I'm pretty sure nobody would ever want to wear those pants again.

THE ALBINO HULK

In the doorway was a massive man, nearly seven feet tall. He wore a suit of startling bright white, every inch of the outfit striated with red tubes that crisscrossed along the seams. It appeared as though a red liquid was running through the tubes. He had on a clear visor, and below that visor was a face that glowed a terrifying bright red. He was bald. His eyes were wide open, tinged the color of burnt amber.

On one hand was a massively padded white glove that looked like it could dislodge a train from its tracks. The other hand was gloveless—and it glowed the bright red of a well-kindled fire. Tendrils of smoke emanated from the exposed hand. Wood from the shattered doorway glowed red, several shards ablaze. Had he done that with his freaky red hand?

"Ezekiel Bartholomew," the man said, his voice

guttural, amplified through what sounded like speakers in the visor.

Not Derek Lance. Ezekiel Bartholomew. He knew who I was.

"Wha...how do you know my name?"

The massive white hulk didn't respond. Instead he crossed the doorway, each footstep causing the floor to tremble. I backed up against the wall. He crossed the foyer in seconds. I was barely up to his shoulders. The gigantic man stood in front of me. Looked me over for a brief moment. Then reared the ungloved, red hand back and...

"HOLY CRAP!" I shouted, diving out of the way a split second before the huge appendage came hurtling forward, lodging itself in the wall right where my head had just been. Ever wondered what a grapefruit would look like after getting hit by a nuclear weapon? I'm pretty sure that's what my head would have resembled had the punch connected.

I rolled out of the way and sprinted into Gertie's living room. The hulking man yanked his fist from the wall, leaving a small fire in its wake. I watched in disbelief. Somehow the man's skin possessed the ability to create spontaneous combustion.

I only had a moment to feel dorky about knowing the term "spontaneous combustion" before the man lumbered after me into the living room. By that time, the fire from the doorway had caught onto the curtains. Flames began to lick at the ceiling.

"Gertie!" I shouted. "Run!"

"Way ahead of you, kid!" I saw Gertie sprint toward the door. Well, *sprint* isn't the right word. No, she *ambled* the best an elderly woman could. I heard a set of car keys jingling in her hand. "Thanks for setting my house on fire, Zeke! Now the insurance company will have no choice but to pay through the nose! Oh, and try to stay alive!"

Then Gertie was gone.

I ran behind the old couch. The ghostlike hulk stopped in front of it.

"Now, hold on a freaking second!" I shouted. "I'm not Derek Lance. I'm Zeke Bartholomew. I'm in the seventh grade. I suck at dodgeball. I got a *C-* on my last social studies test. And I don't have any stupid codes!"

"You know about Operation Songbird," the hulk said. "For that, you cannot live."

I ducked down just as a huge boot sent the couch

hurtling over my head. Oh, sure, best dodgeball move I've made in my life, and of course nobody from school was there to see it.

I scrambled out of the living room and into the kitchen. The white hulk followed me.

On the counter was a rolling pin. I picked it up, turned back to the monster, and hurled it at his face with every ounce of strength I could muster. I let out a manly *PHNEGH!* sound as the rolling pin left my hand.

I watched it fly as if in slow motion—as it harmlessly bounced off the man's visor and plunked to the ground, where it lay, seeming to mock my ineptitude. I turned back to the hulk. A backhand with his gloved fist sent me face-first into the refrigerator.

The blow nearly knocked me unconscious. Woozy, my reflexes were just intact enough to sidestep a punch from the ungloved fist. The fist shattered the fridge, plowing through its metal door.

Suddenly I heard a high-pitched noise so loud that I had to cover my ears. I looked up to see the hulk withdraw his hand from the freezer. He stared at it, the face beneath his visor contorted into a look of pure agony. White steam was pouring off his hand, and small blisters were forming and then popping, a disgusting red ooze flowing out from the burst pustules.

He quickly snapped the glove back over his wounded limb and doubled over in pain. This was my chance.

I ran from the kitchen. The entire house was bathed in red flames. Wooden beams were crashing down around me. I could feel the heat singeing my eyebrows. I coughed as I drew smoke into my lungs. The bashed-in doorway was a ring of fire. I had no choice. The hulk was certainly regrouping somewhere behind me.

"Just like gymnastic class," I said, with a complete lack of confidence, considering I'd once fallen spread-legged on the balance beam, necessitating a daylong stay in the school nurse's station with bruised...never mind.

I closed my eyes. Sucked in one last lungful of air. Then leaped through the fiery doorway.

IT'S A BIRD, IT'S A PLANE, IT'S A...SPARROW?

I landed with a thud, the gravel from Gertie's driveway scraping my arms and face. I lay there for a moment, then sprang back up. I checked my body. Nothing on fire. Nothing appeared to be broken. Unfortunately the same could not be said for Gertie Zimmerman's house.

The roof had sagged in, and pillars of fire raged through the night sky. Smoke billowed into the air. If Gertie hadn't been so happy to be done with the place, I would have felt really, really bad.

Then, without warning, the entire roof collapsed, sending a mountain of ash and sparks into the air. I stepped back, shielding my eyes from the smoldering wreckage.

The hulk. He was still in there. I wasn't sure how to react to the monster's death.

Unluckily for me, I didn't have much time to worry about it.

Several pieces of wood went flying, and out of the wooden mess stepped the monster. My jaw dropped. He paused. Brushed some ash and wood from the white suit. And began heading right back toward me.

I walked backward. The sun was beginning to come up, and I could see the panic in my face reflected in his clear visor. There was no emotion in his eyes. He was going to kill me. Really, really soon.

He clutched his left hand like a bird with an injured wing. But it didn't slow him down. And I had nowhere to run.

Slowly backing up, I held out my hands.

"We can talk about this, right? Why don't you just tell me your dastardly plans first?"

I figured my best chance to get away was to get the monster monologuing—revealing his evil plans in such excruciating, long-winded detail that I could sneak away while he talked about how he was going to destroy humanity, yada yada yada.

Instead, the giant man said nothing. He removed the glove from his uninjured hand. Both his eyes and his clenched fist grew bright red.

I was going to die.

Then, along with my reflection in his visor, I saw something else. A tiny speck that seemed to grow larger, and larger, and larger, until…was that a…person?

Something—or somebody—landed on the white hulk feet-first, knocking the monster flat onto his back. A parachute fluttered to the ground behind me. Like a whirling dervish, this strange person pulled something out of a knapsack. It glittered in the sun. And before I knew what was going on, I saw that a hole had been cut in the monster's visor.

This intruder stepped back. I couldn't see his face, just a mop of auburn hair. The monster struggled to its feet, eyes glaring hatred through his shorn visor.

"Hey, smokey," the stranger said. It was a *girl's* voice! "Eat this."

She tossed a liquid through the visor, which splashed all over the monster's red face. He began to scream, with the same mist and blisters appearing as when he'd punched the freezer.

"Come on, Zeke!" the girl cried out.

"Wait, who—"

She grabbed me by the wrist, and soon we were both sprinting through the woods.

"The liquid nitrogen won't last long," the girl said. "It's an irritant. Like using pepper spray on a normal person."

She could run much, much faster than me. My lungs were sucking air. She didn't seem to even be breaking a sweat.

The girl looked to be about my age. She wore a tight, black uniform-style outfit, molded to her toned body. Her hair was auburn, tied up in the back, and her eyes were a steely blue. There was no fear in them. I tripped on a root. She had to help me up. Yeah, it was pretty clear who the leader of this pack was (hint: not Zeke).

After about ten minutes of running—which I'm pretty sure was the longest single amount of time I've ever spent running—we came to a clearing.

"There's not much time," the girl said. She slung off her knapsack and pulled out some sort of belt-and-strap contraption. She handed me a pair of underwear.

"Why are you giving me underwear?" I said.

"They're not underwear, stupid. It's a harness. Put it on. Your legs go through the strap holes."

"Right. Of course. A harness. I knew that." I put my legs through the straps and buckled the harness around my waist. "Great, now what?"

"Now," she said, pulling me up against her, "we connect." She snapped a few buckles together, and suddenly my harness was connected to hers.

"I'm not sure if I feel comfortable with this."

"Would you feel more comfortable with a fist about three thousand degrees Celsius ramming through your nose with enough force to incinerate your brain stem?"

"No. That would be decidedly less comfortable," I said.

"Smart kid. Now, hang on." The girl pressed a button on a wristband and spoke into it. "Thirty-seven point five north, eighty-two point two west. Go."

"Wait...who are you?"

"I'm Sparrow."

Sparrow pressed another button on her wristband, and a rope line shot into the air, attached to some sort of flashing red balloon. A signal The rope rose high into the air, a faint gray strand in the orange of early morning. Once the rope went taut, I heard the deafening noise of a plane approaching us. Louder than I'd ever heard a plane before.

I looked up. A plane *was* approaching, barely a hundred feet off the ground. And this wasn't your normal passenger plane, but what looked to be a small aircraft.

There was no cockpit, nothing for anyone to see out of. It was unmanned. Cool.

A pair of scissorlike talons emerged from the front of the plane, which was flying at the same altitude as the balloon. I understood what Sparrow's plan was.

"This can't be a good idea," I said.

"Stop worrying. I've done this a hundred times."

I turned my head around to look at her. "Who *are* you?"

Before she could answer, I heard a crashing sound and the white hulk appeared in the clearing. He was wielding a tree trunk the size of most motorboats. And the tree trunk was on fire. I could see blisters and red pus running down his face through the broken visor. And not that I had much experience with it, but I had to think that anytime somebody came at you wielding a giant flaming tree trunk, it wasn't a good thing.

"Uh, Sparrow..." I said, turning back. There was a slight trace of fear in her eyes. It didn't exactly make me feel better.

The monster ran toward us, with the tree pulled back like a baseball bat. Then, just as he swung his weapon, the plane caught hold of our rope line and yanked us high into the air. I felt a gust of wind as the massive tree trunk missed bashing my legs in by about a millimeter.

We were whisked away, dangling by the line as the plane tore through the air. My hair flapped about as I watched the ground disappear below us. The harness held tight, and thankfully I'd already thrown up all the spaghetti, because I don't think the human body—or at least *my* body—was built for this.

Sparrow pressed another button on her wristband and the rope began to recoil, pulling us up toward the plane.

"Stay calm," Sparrow said. "We have a lot to talk about."

"Right. Yeah. Lots to talk about. Hey, um, Sparrow?"

"Yeah?"

"Is there supposed to be a giant flaming tree trunk flying at us?"

Sparrow looked down. She saw what I saw. A giant flaming tree trunk flying at us. I could tell by her lack of response that this wasn't an everyday occurrence.

"Watch out!" she cried, twisting our attached bodies out of the way. The trunk barely missed us—but slammed into the plane's right-side engine, causing an explosion that sent metal and wood flying all around us.

The loss of the engine caused the plane to bank to the left. I heard myself scream as the swirling plane dragged us with it, black exhaust smoke enveloping us.

"We're going down!" Sparrow shouted.

Not something you like to hear from your supposed rescuer.

The plane kept swirling about, as we hung from the rescue rope like a pair of fish at the end of a crazy person's reel.

"We need to cut loose!" said Sparrow. "I can't…I can't reach it!"

"Reach what?" I yelled.

"In my boot, there's a knife. We need to cut the cord!"

"Won't we, like, fall to our deaths?"

"How is that different from what we're doing now?" She had a fair point. "See if you can reach it. Hurry, Zeke!"

I doubled over, the harness across my stomach preventing me from reaching too far. I could see the handle of a knife protruding from a sheath in Sparrow's boot. I had to reach it; otherwise we would go down in flames with the destroyed plane.

"Sparrow in!" the girl said into her wristband. "Subject

has been acquired, but we are going down. Repeat, we are going down."

The plane was spiraling out of control. Below us, trees spun like a whirlpool, and for about the umpteenth time today I felt nauseous. I could touch the handle of the knife with my finger—but couldn't reach far enough to grip it.

We were running out of time. The plane was going down.

"What's taking so long?" Sparrow shouted, her words barely registering above the noise.

"I can't reach it," I said. There was only one way to save our lives. I hoped Sparrow was as strong as she looked. "I need you to hold on to me."

"What? You're snapped in."

"I know," I said. "I'm going to unhook myself from you."

"Are you crazy?" she said.

"Are you strong enough?"

"Under normal circumstances, yes. With enough g-forces to tear the stripes off a zebra, I don't know."

"Well, either way, if I don't do this, we're both a splotch on the ground somewhere. Grab my pants. I'm going to lean over."

I waited until Sparrow had clutched my waist tightly. Then I took a deep breath, telling myself, *This is just like Space Mountain. This is just like Space Mountain.* Of course, I avoided thinking the part about how on Space Mountain you're shackled in with that massive metal bar to keep you from falling off the ride.

I unsnapped the first hook that connected me to Sparrow. I keeled forward…but she caught me. Then I unhooked the second, lurching forward even more. My head and most of my body were now tilted toward the ground. I lunged again for the knife, gripping it with my thumb and forefinger. Still not enough. It was wedged in there good and tight.

"Last one!" I shouted.

"You're crazy!" she said. This coming from a girl who had just parachuted onto a superhuman monster and then tried to have us rappelled into the air by an unmanned aircraft. Yeah. I was *clearly* the crazy one in this equation.

I unhooked the last clasp and felt myself suddenly free-falling. Then I stopped. Sparrow had me. But from the noises she was making, it wasn't for very long.

I reached down and pulled the knife free. It was a big, scary-looking thing with a serrated edge. My dad once freaked out when I bought a Swiss Army knife. If he'd seen this baby, his head would have exploded.

"You're going to need to do it!" she shouted. "If I let go, you'll fall!"

That was all the convincing I needed. Hoisting myself up, careful not to slice anything human, I reached up high and placed the serrated edge against the rope.

"Nice and easy and—" Sparrow said, but before she could finish, I'd made one quick slice right through the line, and suddenly we were hurtling toward the ground.

"Hang on to me!" she shouted. I clasped my hands around Sparrow's waist. There were rocks and trees and road and cars directly beneath us. I didn't really want to know what it would feel like to hit any one of them at that speed. The wind whipped at my hair, my cheeks flapping with the air pressure. We clung to each other like two stapled pieces of paper.

"Three, two, one, now!" Sparrow pulled a cord on her knapsack, and a bright yellow parachute opened above us. Our fall was halted. The parachute caught the wind. We whooshed over the cars and the woods, heading right for...an open lake.

Down, down, down we went, until the parachute

splashed down in the water. I swam to the surface, gasping for air. I didn't see anyone else, just the parachute spread out across the lake.

"Sparrow!" I cried out. Had she come up? Had the impact knocked her unconscious? I dove back under the water, searching frantically in the murky gloom. I could barely see five feet in front of me. There was no way I could cover enough of the lake to find her. Where could she be?

"Sparrow!" I yelled again, only this time I was underwater and nearly puked up a gallon of the stuff when I got to the surface. *No yelling underwater, Zeke.*

After ten minutes of swimming and searching, there was still no sign of my savior. I didn't know what else to do. So I swam to the bank and hauled my wet carcass out. I was getting really tired of pulling myself out of bodies of water.

I stared out at the blue expanse. The yellow parachute drifted for a few more minutes, then folded up on itself and sank.

"Sparrow..." I whispered, head in my hands. "I'M SO SORRY!"

"Sorry for what?" a voice behind me asked.

I turned around. Sparrow was standing there, squeezing water from her hair.

"You're alive!" I ran over to her and threw my arms around her.

"Easy there, Swamp Thing." I backed off.

"I thought you were dead."

"You think a plane explosion and an emergency crash landing in a lake would kill me?" Sparrow said, laughing.

Her laughter unnerved me. Any one of a thousand things could have killed me, maimed me, burned me, exploded me, or beat me up real good today. And she was laughing about it. It felt like the time I won a fourth-grade chess tournament, only to then get beat up by the kid who won the karate tournament being held next door.

"By the way, I found your pants." She held up Gertie's husband's soaked trousers. I looked down. My tighty whiteys were plastered to my pale legs.

I grabbed the trousers and put them on angrily. "Why the heck do I keep losing my pants? I swear, this is some kind of pants conspiracy."

Sparrow held up a finger and whispered, "*Shh.*"

"Come on," she said, tapping her wristband. "It's

destroyed. Unbelievable. With all the technology at our disposal, you'd think they could waterproof the ComLet."

"ComLet?"

"Communications bracelet. Most of us call it the ComLet. But the wusses who aren't secure enough in their masculinity to admit that they wear a bracelet just call it the MultiPurp. Either way, without this we're in a bit of a bind."

"Who are you talking about?" I said. "I don't know what you're talking about with this ComMultiPerp Hot Pocket thing. Speak English."

Sparrow sighed. She walked over to me. "Calm down."

I gritted my teeth. "I am calm. And considering I've been semi-kidnapped, almost killed by a giant white gorilla person, almost incinerated in a plane crash, and lost my pants *twice* in the past two days, I'm as calm as could possibly be expected. But if I don't get some answers *now*, whatever your name is, I might lose that calm and just go freaky nuts on you."

"Freaky nuts?" she asked incredulously.

"Yeah. Freaky nuts." This did not sound nearly as intimidating as I thought it would.

"Okay. You want some answers?"

"I think I'm entitled to them."

"You want answers?"

"I want the truth!"

"You can't handle the truth!" Sparrow said.

"I think I've heard that somewhere before," I said.

"Here's what we know," Sparrow said. "For years we have been tracking a massive criminal enterprise. Their funding has been in the billions, and they have enough manpower and firepower to take over a small country. The enterprise was run by a man named Le Carré."

"I know that name," I said. "The goons who took me, they said he was going to be real upset if I didn't give them the codes."

Sparrow furrowed her brow. She did not like hearing that.

"I work for an agency called SNURP. The Strategic National Underground Reconnaissance Project."

"You're a spy," I said.

"To put it bluntly, yes. We are spies. As you may have guessed, my code name is Sparrow."

"Cool code name."

"Thank you. Anyway, ten years ago SNURP began development on a project called SirEebro. SirEebro was, in effect, a massive transmission device. It could take any sound wave and 'hijack' the signal, encoding it with subliminal sound waves."

"That sounds like brainwashing. Like heavy metal records that secretly tell you to go eat bunnies or something."

Sparrow stared at me. "Are you, like, brain damaged or something?"

"Not that I know of. But isn't it kind of like that?"

"In simple terms? Like very basic simple terms that even a child could understand?"

"I'm a lot smarter than you think," I said.

She looked at me, trying to discern whether I was merely saying it to defend myself. Or if I was, in fact, capable of greater deduction than she thought.

Then I hiccupped.

"Sorry. Happens sometimes when I'm nervous."

"Maybe you're right," Sparrow said. "Maybe you're not just some kid living in small-town nowhere who can't tell his butt from his nose. We'll see. Because your life is going to depend on it."

"Whoa, hold on there, Robin."

"Sparrow."

"Whatever. I'm done with all this spy stuff. I fell off a

bridge, almost drowned, nearly got killed by some giant... *thing*...and just fell from an airplane *that I was dangling from on a grappling hook*. I have homework due Monday. A problem set for algebra. And I haven't done any of the reading. I'm going home."

"If you go home, your father will die."

I stopped in my tracks.

"What did you just say?"

"Your father. Jonah Bartholomew. Age forty-two, currently employed as a tax attorney at the law firm of Holt, Lester, and Carol."

"How do you know that? How do you know about my dad?"

"We know everything about you, Zeke. The moment you used Gertie Zimmerman's phone, we were able to track you down and find out everything about you in less time than it takes you to Google 'boogers.' Your mother, Sandra, passed away six years ago. Your father has an account on three dating websites but hasn't updated them in over two years."

"Stop talking about my dad," I said, my teeth gnashing against each other.

Sparrow held up her hands. "I'm not saying this to

upset you, Zeke. I'm only saying this because everything we know, they know."

"Who is 'they'? This Le Carré guy?"

"Yes. And Ragnarok."

"Who the heck is Ragnarok?"

"Ragnarok is that *thing* that nearly killed you back there. Ragnarok's real name is Richard Knox. He was a world-famous geologist and seismologist, not to mention world-class triathlete. He was in a plane, flying solo, surveying a volcano in Iceland, and was in the blast zone when the volcano blew. His plane went down. The wreckage was found, but Knox was not. One year later, he was seen at a secret rehabilitation facility in Switzerland. His skin was ashen, white, and tubes were hooked up all over his body. Red liquid was seen coursing through the tubes."

"Just like on his suit," Zeke said.

"Yes. The exposure to the volcanic blast changed Knox's thermal temperature. He cannot exist at temperatures below two hundred degrees Celsius. That red liquid you saw is pure volcanic magma."

"Those tubes. They would need to be made of a special material. It would need to be both flexible and anti-corrosive. Likely some sort of aluminum/steel hybrid."

"Maybe you're not as dumb as I thought," Sparrow said.

"Don't give yourself a headache with all these compliments. That's why when he touched ice cubes it was like he'd suffered instant frostbite."

"Anyway, I'm not telling you this to scare you. It's fact. A few months ago, SirEebro was stolen from a secured armored carrier while en route to the SNURP headquarters. They were blindsided and taken out by laser rifles, an incredibly advanced technology. These weren't regular thieves. We believe somebody tipped off a dangerous enemy."

"What do you mean 'enemy'?" I asked.

"We weren't sure. At least not until we found you."

"Wonderful," I said. "Happy to be the key to this insane puzzle."

"The scientists at SNURP were smart enough to install a safeguard into SirEebro. The device itself is harmless, unless…"

"Unless they have the program codes."

"That's right."

"So whoever stole it wasn't able to get the codes."

"Correct. We didn't keep them with the device."

"Which means they needed somebody from inside SNURP who had access to the codes."

"Exactly."

"And so those people who took me the other night, they thought I was Derek Lance, because...Derek Lance has those codes."

Sparrow nodded solemnly.

"Which means that Derek Lance is an agent of SNURP."

"*Was* an agent of SNURP. He was the greatest young spy our agency had ever seen. A few months back Lance began acting strange. He was always a bit of a weirdo to begin with."

"Seriously. Who wears sunglasses to class?"

"That's not what I meant. It's not usual for a twelve-year-old to have a god complex. But Lance would always say that god had a Derek Lance complex. We believe he stole the codes and was planning to sell them to Le Carré. You happened to be in the wrong place at the wrong time, Zeke. And now, even though you don't have the codes, you know about SirEebro."

"And Operation Songbird," I said.

Sparrow looked at me strangely. "Operation what?"

"Songbird. The agents—whoever they were—the Brooks Brothers guys who picked me up, they talked about an Operation Songbird that would go into effect in twenty-four hours. Wait, no, technically that was last night, so it would be in about," I checked my watch, "twelve hours."

Sparrow looked concerned. "That is very not good. What did they tell you about Operation Songbird?"

"That's, that's really it. I don't know anything else. I just want to go home and for my dad to be left alone."

"That's not possible. You're in this, Zeke. The best we can hope for right now is to keep you and your father alive."

"Best we can hope for?"

She looked at me. "We don't make promises."

I sighed. What else could I have done? Sat back and let that boiling hulk ruin my life? I wasn't helpless. I'd gotten an *A* in physics and chemistry. Provided I didn't have to outmaneuver dodgeballs or avoid wedgies, I felt I had something to offer.

"We need to find out where the goons were taking me. Le Carré's headquarters. That's where we'll get to the bottom of Operation Songbird."

"Agreed. But my ComLet is busted. I need to—"

I ripped the ComLet off of Sparrow's wrist.

"Hey!" she shouted. "Give that back!"

She reached for it. I pulled it away. I opened the battery pack and…*oof*…was not prepared as Sparrow planted the heel of her palm right into my stomach. The wind flew from my lungs faster than a hurled tree trunk.

I collapsed into a heap, wheezing.

"I was just…*cough*…trying…*wheeze*…to tell you… *hack*…I can fix it."

Her eyes perked up. "Um, really?"

"Yes…*sputter*…have parts…*groan*…at my lab."

"Your lab? What are we waiting for? Let's go!"

Clearly Sparrow wasn't big on apologies. Instead she picked me up, hurled me up on her shoulders like a log, and began to walk. Either she was as strong as an ox, or I needed to eat more meat.

I managed to squirm out of her grasp. "I can walk," I said as my breath returned.

"Just trying to move us along. We don't have much time if those goons were right about Operation Songbird."

"Where are you even going?"

"To the road," she said evenly. "We're going to steal a car."

A THIEF IN THE DAYLIGHT

Sparrow wasn't kidding.

The nearest road was about three miles away. It was a remote one-lane road, with trees on either side and nary a stoplight or stop sign in sight. Ten minutes passed between each car. We tried to hitchhike, but since it wasn't the 1960s nobody stopped for us.

"This is useless," I said. "We'd be better off walking back."

"We're about twenty miles from your neighborhood. If we walk, by the time we get back, Operation Songbird will already have gone into effect. Don't be stupid."

"Yeah, SNURP didn't bother to make your oh-so-important, crummy spy bracelet waterproof. And you call me stupid."

"Car!" Sparrow yelled. Approaching us was a beat-up blue station wagon, the kind of car that was worth more as scrap than as a vehicle. It sputtered and shook. I laughed.

"Feel bad for the poor schmo who...*oof*."

Before I could get the next word out, Sparrow had pushed me into the middle of the road. The car screeched and stopped, smoke billowing from the exhaust. The driver's eyes went wide, and he screamed so loud I could see his tonsils vibrating.

The car came to a stop four feet from my nose.

Sparrow immediately ran over to the driver's side door. The man got out. He was wearing a mesh trucker cap. Ironic since his car had as much in common with a truck as I did. His eyes were bloodshot and his face was ripe with black stubble.

"I...I didn't see you there, kid. You okay?"

"Give me your address," Sparrow said.

"Excuse me?"

"Your address. Give it to me."

"What for?"

"Because we're stealing your car and I need to make sure you get reimbursed. I'd say this car is worth about five hundred dollars. We'll send you a thousand."

"This was a setup? You ain't taking Bessie nowhere, you crazy bandits!"

"Your car has a name? So cliché. Fine. Two thousand.

You complain any more, and I'll dislocate every finger on your right hand and then insult your mother."

The driver looked at Sparrow as if she'd sprouted two heads.

"She'll do it," I said. "She pushed me in front of your car."

"Yeah. Right." He took out his wallet and handed Sparrow a business card. "You'll really pay me for Bessie?"

"Darn right. We may be spies, but we're not thieves."

She took the key from Bessie's owner, waited until he moved to the side of the road, then slipped behind the wheel.

"Come on, Zeke."

"Are you crazy? You're, what, eleven?"

"Twelve. And you're a nerd, and here we are. Come on."

Cautiously I opened the passenger door and got in. I buckled the seat belt, then looked around for Velcro, Krazy Glue, or anything else that could keep me attached to the seat.

"Hang on," she said.

"To what?" I replied.

Sparrow didn't wait for an answer.

Within seconds, we were speeding down the road at

approximately the same speed as the average space shuttle launch. Around the time we crossed into Mach 4 I realized Sparrow was hugging every curve, rounding every turn fluidly.

"Have you done this before?" I said.

"No. First time."

"Really?"

"No."

"You know, you don't *always* need to make fun of me."

"Where's the fun in that?"

"You're a…jerkface."

"Nice one."

We made the twenty-mile drive in about ten minutes. Or thirty seconds. Either way, it was about ten times faster than we would have made it if my dad (aka Slowpoke McBadDriver) had been behind the wheel.

Soon I began to recognize my neighborhood. And just as soon as I did, I also began to recognize the thick plumes of black smoke gushing from under the car's hood.

"Uh, Sparrow. I think you pushed Bessie too hard."

"She can take it."

One minute later the smoke was followed by a bright, loud spark. And then Bessie caught on fire.

Sparrow slammed on the brakes. Thankfully my seat belt kept me in place. We leaped out of the car, just as tendrils of flame began to blacken the rusty blue paint.

"She was a good girl," I said. "And went out in style."

"Classy eulogy. Let's go. Do you know where we are?"

I looked around. The town swimming pool was just a few blocks away, and I recognized the old run-down movie theater that hadn't seen business since people called it pop instead of soda.

"There," I said, pointing at the Brian Brooks Little League Field a few blocks away. It was a beautiful field, with lush green grass and dirt as pure as, well, dirt could be. Even though I wasn't much of an athlete, I would lie in the outfield during the off season to read, stare at the clouds, and wonder what people braver than me were doing at that very moment. Right now, though, I had no time for daydreaming.

"The baseball field? Your lab is on the baseball field?"

"Not on," I said. "Under."

I jogged over to the field and opened the gate to the ballpark. I inhaled deeply. I loved that smell. Sparrow followed, hesitant.

"Where are we going?"

"Just come on. I was out here a few years ago when I noticed that shed out in the distance," I said. "I'd never seen anybody go in or out. It was just *there.* One day I got curious. It had an old rusty lock on it. I broke it off with an aluminum bat. And found this."

On the door was a combination lock. I'd put it there. As far as I knew, nobody else had even tried to get in after me. It was hiding in plain sight.

I entered the combination, 5-2-8, May 28, the birthday of Ian Fleming, the man who created James Bond. I took off the lock and yanked open the creaky door.

"This is it?" she said.

"Sometimes you need to look closer," I said. "Things can be more than they seem."

Inside the shed was a water fountain. It was caked in grime and sludge. Next to it was a grate that measured about eighteen by twelve inches. That was it. Nothing else. Except the dime.

Inside the water dish on the fountain was a run-of-the-mill dime. I'd left it there the first time I found the shed, knowing what it was used for.

I took the dime and knelt down. One by one I inserted it into the small slot at the top of each of the four screws holding down the grate. A little elbow grease and the grate was free. I pulled it off the opening and gently placed it to the side of the fountain.

"Let's go."

"Down there?" Sparrow said. She peered into the darkness, appearing hesitant. Strange for a girl who had just parachuted away from a damaged aircraft. My dad has a friend, Phil Bushwick, who served in the navy. Big, strong guy who looks like he wears his skin three sizes too small. Phil is afraid of frogs. I mean, once I brought a live frog home, and when he saw it, Phil, who was having a beer with my dad, fell over backward in his chair, cracked his head on the floor, and ended up in the hospital with a concussion. Maybe long, dark tunnels were Sparrow's frog.

"You can wait here," I said. "I'll take the ComLet and go myself."

This appeared to anger Sparrow. "I'd rather fall into a vat of boiling acid. Let's go, tunnel rat. You first."

"No need to be so dramatic. Come on. " I climbed into the grate opening.

There were old metal footholds on the side where sewage workers must have climbed up and down at one point. Step by step I made my way down the ladder into the damp, smelly darkness. I'd made this trip many times, often with backpacks full of stuff. I felt a slight surge of pride when I saw Sparrow daintily making her way down, pausing every few seconds to check below her. For the first time all day, I felt like the braver person.

"Careful," I said, helping her the last few steps. A narrow stream of water flowed through the middle of the tunnel. The walls were slick rock, slimy, and the whole place smelled dank. There was barely any light. But I knew the way by heart. "Follow me."

I led the way, Sparrow's shoes clacking on the rocks behind me. I'd memorized the path a long time ago. One hundred thirty-seven paces forward—to the T-junction. At the T-junction, we made a left. Forty-two paces to the next junction. From there we made a right.

"I hope you know what you're doing," Sparrow whispered.

"Shh," I said. "You'll make me lose focus and then we'll be lost."

"Lost? Are you kidding? Where are we, Zeke?"

"Calm down. I'm kidding. I know exactly where we are. Geez, were you born in a dark tunnel or something?"

Sparrow didn't respond. I looked back. Something I'd said had clearly touched a nerve, because she was staring down at the rocks. Water whooshed between us. The mystery of Sparrow was deepening. I wanted to ask what the problem was, but if the goons were right, there wasn't much time before Operation Songbird—whatever it was—took effect.

At the latest junction, we took the roundabout until we came to a long, dark corridor. I remembered the very first time I'd come down here. It was three years earlier. Kyle had finished a little league game. He was pitching. At the time, he was only nine inches or so taller than everybody else. His blazing fastball made the other boys in our grade flail like they were swatting invisible flies. After the game, while the teams were shaking hands, one of the opposing kids tripped Kyle. He went down like a broken branch.

Everyone laughed at him. Even the kids on his own team. The kids he'd just helped win. I was in the stands with my dad. I felt awful watching it. Kyle lay there, embarrassed. Finally the kids all left. I told my dad I'd meet him at home. I went out to the pitcher's mound, where Kyle was sitting with his face in his glove. I told him he didn't need those jerks. He didn't say anything. We spent the afternoon talking. He said he wanted to play baseball in college, maybe the pros, but didn't think he could handle it if things were like this. He said he didn't want to be a geek forever. I told him that the kids who were geeks in school ended up the most successful people ever. Bill Gates was a geek. That guy who invented Facebook was a geek. George Lucas? Steven Spielberg? Mega-geeks. I told him he should be proud to be a geek—because we would inherit the earth. Or at least invent cool new software.

We walked around the outfield and eventually stumbled across the shed. Kyle said sometimes he wished he could crawl into a dark hole and disappear. That's when I took the dime out of my pocket and said, "Now's our chance."

I unscrewed the grate, and the rest is history.

Eighty-four paces after the roundabout, Sparrow and I came to a door. It was barely visible in the gloom. Kyle and I had found the door by accident. It was the greatest discovery of our lives. Kyle had put a large Master Lock padlock on it. The combination was 9-29-14.

"Are you ready?" I asked.

"For what?" Sparrow replied. "More murk?"

I ignored the comment. I gripped the lock and entered

the combination. It released. I removed it and put it in my pocket.

Then I gently pushed the door open. Sparrow's eyes opened wide.

"Whoa…this is…"

"The GeekDen," I said. "The name is a work in progress."

"Progress," Sparrow said absently. "Right."

She stepped into the GeekDen and took in her surroundings. I felt a faint burst of pride as she surveyed the cave Kyle and I had built over the last few years.

The walls were lined with dozens of shelves, each of which was piled high with circuitry, wiring, and various battery packs. A workbench at the far end held every kind of tool imaginable, all laid out as neatly as a surgeon's table. A bookshelf was piled high with manuals, glossaries, instruction books, and how-to videos. Blueprints were tacked to the walls, each design one of our own making.

There were screws, bolts, wires, tubes, cylinders, beakers, and everything a growing mad scientist could possibly want. It had taken Kyle and me weeks and weeks to gather everything, transporting it step by careful step down that dark hole and through the damp sewers. This GeekDen was everything I couldn't do out in the open. In here I was allowed to be myself. In here I wasn't Zeke Bartholomew, First-Class Nerdzilla. Here I was Zeke Bartholomew, Superspy.

I turned the ComLet over in my hands. It was a fantastic piece of equipment, something that would have been impossible to manufacture given my relatively meager access to these kind of high-tech materials. Still, despite its technological advances, the ComLet was assembled in a pretty primitive fashion. Aside from the lack of waterproofing, the circuitry was all wrong. It was too bulky, too heavy. If I had the resources Sparrow did, I could make the most kicking ComLet ever.

"Give me a minute," I said. I took the ComLet over to the workbench. I unscrewed the battery chamber and pried open the circuitry board. The batteries were a little waterlogged and would need to be replaced. I didn't recognize the type of batteries it used—but I could work around that. The wiring was another matter.

Much of the circuitry board was fried. The wires had grown corrosive. Diodes ruined. I pulled a box off the shelf, rifled through it, and spilled a mess of pieces onto the table. I could feel Sparrow's eyes watching me intently. I had no intention of letting her down.

I put on a pair of magnifying glasses to get a better look at the circuit board close up. It didn't look good.

The first step was replacing the destroyed wiring. With a pair of tweezers, I gently removed the burned wires, including pieces stuck to the board. I opened up a fresh toothbrush from a box and dipped it in rubbing alcohol. Using my makeshift cleaner, I brushed away any residue and scraped off any bits of metal and wiring that had fastened themselves to the board. Any debris I threw into a small box. Some of it might be able to be repurposed later. Then I took a soldering iron and replaced the damaged wires with fresh ones.

It was a painstaking, arduous process, not made easier at all by the fact that Sparrow spent the entire time leaning over my shoulder and asking unhelpful questions like, "Are you sure you're not breaking it?"

"Your ComLet fell from a plane, landed in a lake, and short-circuited. And you're asking me if *I'm* breaking it?"

Finally she got the picture and backed off a bit. I got the sense that Sparrow was not used to anybody other than herself having control over a situation. And it was just as strange for me. The only situation I tend to have control over is how much milk I pour into my cereal in the morning.

Half an hour after I began, I'd done all I could. The wires were replaced. The board cleaned of all residue. I still had no idea if any of this would work—but there was only one way to find out.

I handed the newly repaired ComLet back to Sparrow. "Give it a whirl."

She took it from me and turned it over in her hands. "Let's see just what kind of whiz kid you are, Zeke."

Sparrow strapped the device back onto her wrist, then held a pair of buttons on the outer rim. For a moment, nothing happened. No sounds, nothing. My heart sank. Sparrow looked dejected. Then…a light began to blink. It was yellow. I pointed at it.

"What…what does that mean?"

Sparrow's eyes lit up. "That means it's recalibrating. It's what happens after you restore the ComLet to its original settings. It means it's working."

There was a faint humming sound. The yellow light began to blink, and then it turned green. And once it turned green, the computer inside activated. It lit up in front of us. I couldn't tell what was beaming brighter—me or the ComLet.

"It works!" Sparrow cried out.

I smiled. "Of course it does. That's what I do." I had mentally given the ComLet about a fifty-fifty chance of actually working, but I didn't tell Sparrow that.

"This is incredible, Zeke," she said, toggling around with the newly fixed ComLet. "How did you learn how to do all this?"

"I taught myself."

She looked up from the hardware.

"Seriously?"

"Um…yeah. I've always had a knack for gadgets and stuff. Always wanted to make my own things. But science and physics teachers never really teach you more than what will help you pass pop quizzes. I wanted to go beyond that. I wanted to be like Q."

"Q?"

"You know, from the James Bond movies. The guy who makes all the cool things, like grappling hooks that look like cocktail napkins and lasers built into rabbits' feet."

"I must have missed those movies."

I laughed long and deep until my sides hurt. Then I stopped. "Wait...you're serious?"

"I never had time for movies. I was out actually saving the world."

"Yeah. I see how that could eat into your free time."

Sparrow fiddled with her ComLet. "We need to go back to the surface. It doesn't get good reception down here."

"Are you kidding me? Who manufactures your devices, a blind marmot? I could build a cell phone that gets five-bar reception down here in one day, and SNURP, with all its resources, can't do it?"

I could see Sparrow beginning to boil under the collar. No sense arguing. We'd need to get back to the surface anyway. Hopefully at that point we could get her ComSuckLet working and figure out how to stop Operation Songbird.

"Let's go," she said, and we both turned back to leave the GeekDen.

"Oh, crap," I said.

Standing there in the doorway was Kyle.

"Hey, uh, Zeke," he said. "Who the heck is *she*, and why did you let her in here?"

NOT-SO-SECRET SERVICE

"I'm Zeke's cousin. Stephanie."

Sparrow responded without a moment's hesitation. It led me to believe she'd been caught in predicaments like this before and had the lie well rehearsed. Sadly, I did not.

"Your cousin?" Kyle asked, eyes narrowed. "I thought your aunt lived in North Dakota."

"She does," I stammered. "They're visiting."

"And didn't you tell me you couldn't stand your cousin Dougie? Didn't he smell like kitty litter or something?"

"Mixed with bacon," I replied.

"Yeah. Bacon. I don't remember you mentioning a girl cousin."

"What, do I need to explain my whole life to you? Who are you, my boss? Boss Kyle? Huh? What's your problem anyway?"

Penalty on Zeke: being way too defensive.

"Take it easy," Kyle said. He was nearly as tall as the GeekDen ceiling and practically had to hunch over so as not to scrape his head on the rocks. "Look, I don't really care. But you weren't in school today. I called your house; your dad is freaking out. He said you weren't home last night. Cops are everywhere looking for you."

"Cops?" Sparrow said, suddenly interested in the conversation.

"Yeah. I stopped by your place, Zeke. Cops have been talking to your dad all morning. He said you two had dinner, and that's the last he remembers seeing you. Where've you been, dude? The whole town is freaking out like it's under alien attack. It's actually kinda exciting. Like our town won the Super Bowl or something."

I sank backward, finding a stool, and sighed. Cops everywhere. Looking for me. My dad a nervous wreck. He'd always been protective, especially after my mom died, and my heart broke thinking about the grief this had likely caused him. How could I have been so selfish? Getting into that car like I was some stupid child being offered candy. I'd seen so many movies and read so many spy novels that I'd foolishly begun to think I really was one. And it had brought my father heartache and exposed him to people far more dangerous than anything I could have ever imagined.

This wasn't a game. There wouldn't be any end credits. It was time to end this. It was time to go back to being Zeke Bartholomew, Übernerd. That's who I was. That's all I was.

"Come on," I said to Kyle. "Let's go."

"Wait," Sparrow said, grabbing hold of my arm. "Where do you think you're going?"

"Home, to my dad," I said. "Look, I don't know anything. And if there are cops everywhere, we'll be safe until this whole thing blows over. You have your wristband back and working. You can handle this. Nice seeing you again, 'Stephanie.'"

"You're not thinking this through," Sparrow whispered through gritted teeth. She was staring at Kyle, clearly not wanting to talk any specifics around him. I was glad she felt that way—enough people in my life were in danger because of me. "That 'appointment' is in just a few hours," she said. "I need you there. I'm all alone on this."

I looked back at Sparrow. I didn't know what she wanted from me, or what she needed me for.

"It totally is appointment viewing, I know," Kyle said. "I can't wait."

"What are you talking about?" I asked him.

"Have you gone brain dead? The concert. Tonight at eight o'clock. The debut music video."

"What music video?" Sparrow said.

"Duh," Kyle said. "Penny Bowers and Jimmy Peppers. PB&J. They're introducing the first single from their new album. It's supposed to be, like, the most-watched event in TV history. Our whole school will be watching. Every kid in every school will be watching. Every kid in the world will be watching, and every parent who pretends to not like them. The news predicts more people will watch this new video than the moon landing."

Sparrow and I looked at each other. We were thinking the same thing.

"Are you thinking…" she said, her voice full of trepidation.

"I am."

"Then…"

"I agree. We need to go get sandwiches."

She looked at me like I'd just farted drumsticks.

"Sandwiches. That was a joke," I said. "I know. PB&J. Operation Songbird. The timing seems to make sense."

Sparrow spun around to look at Kyle. "How many people are going to be watching this video, did you say?"

"I don't know," Kyle said. "Their last video supposedly was watched by, like, a hundred million people. And everyone expects this one to be bigger. If you're not watching it, you're a giant loser. And nobody wants to be the only one in school the next day who didn't see it."

"Hundreds of millions of people…" Sparrow said, her voice trembling.

"Maybe more," I said.

"You told me that this SirEebro device, that it could 'hijack' sound waves. Use them to embed subliminal sounds or other things."

Sparrow spoke in an emotionless tone. The enormity of what was happening was reaching her. "It was designed to use on our enemies. To hijack their communications systems. So that radio broadcasts, television signals could be commandeered. We could control what people thought, how they reacted. But it was never used. It was deemed by the Pentagon to be too unethical. Too dangerous. That's why it was being transported to SNURP headquarters. We were going to study it, not use it."

"Well, somebody is about to use it. Le Carré is going to hijack the PB&J broadcast and brainwash hundreds of millions of people. He's going to turn the entire world into brain-dead zombies at his control."

"Uh, Zeke?" Kyle said. I'd totally forgot he was standing there. "What are you two talking about?"

HE WAS WAITING FOR US

2:43 p.m.

Five hours and seventeen minutes until something really, really bad happens, and I don't even want to think about, because I have kind of a weak stomach...

"We need to find where Le Carré is planning to broadcast from and stop him," Sparrow said. She threw open the door and began to run through the sewers. Kyle was standing there, looking like a hurricane had just passed him by.

"Wait...um...Stephanie!" I shouted. It felt silly continuing this ruse, considering the fate of the free-brained world was at stake. But enough people had already gotten in trouble because of me, and if I could keep Kyle out of it any more than he already was, I would do that.

I ran after Sparrow, who'd already turned the corner.

The wrong corner.

I didn't know the sewers well enough that if she got lost we could find our way back.

Enough with the games. We didn't have time for this.

"Sparrow!" I cried out. I couldn't see her. And the sound of feet splashing could have come from anywhere. Why couldn't she just wait? What was it with all these spies and their lack of patience? They seriously needed to just lie down on a beach somewhere and read a trashy magazine or something.

"Zeke!" a voice cried out. It was Kyle. He'd followed us into the sewers. Of course he had. Sparrow and I had been talking some secret mumbo jumbo about the world ending. Who wouldn't be curious?

"Kyle!" I called back. Just great. Ahead of me was Sparrow, running off into who-knows-where, and behind me was Kyle, who was surely confused beyond belief. Aside from that, we couldn't have Kyle going out and telling the whole world about what he'd just heard. Not that anybody would believe him.

Yes, um, I think there's a massive global conspiracy involving a teeny-bopper band and brainwashing, and, um, my friend Zeke, who has pretty much never done anything more strenuous than roll the dice in a game of Dungeons and Dragons, is somehow involved in it.

Yeah. I could see a cop taking that *real* seriously.

Still, if my dad's life was in danger, so was Kyle's. Even if nobody sane believed him, there were some insane people out there clearly willing to do some horrific stuff to keep their secrets hidden. Sparrow had saved me because SNURP needed me. It was up to me to make sure Kyle returned safe and sound to his awkward, gangly self.

Sparrow was strong, tough. She could take care of herself for the time being.

I backtracked through the sewer toward Kyle.

"Kyle!" I cried out again. I ran around the corner, smack-dab into Kyle. We both fell over onto the cobblestone.

"Dude, what's going on? Who is that girl, really?"

"She's my…aw, never mind. Come on, we need to go."

I grabbed Kyle's arm and began to pull him in the direction of the exit. To my surprise, he yanked back.

"Hold on, Zeke. I've known you for ten years, and I've never seen you like this. And I don't think you've ever lied to me. So don't start now. What the heck is going on, and who is that girl you keep calling Stephanie?"

I turned to Kyle, a swell of guilt rising in me.

"You're right," I said. "I don't want to lie to you. So don't make me. Just please, Kyle, trust me on this and follow me. I'll explain everything when I get a chance, but right now there's no time."

"Is this some sort of freaky spy role-playing game?" Kyle said. He laughed and clapped his hands together like he'd just solved a puzzle. "I bet that's it. She's some girl you met online and you're both pretending to be, what, MI6? CIA? FBI? Men in Black?"

"Dude, like I said, I won't lie to you…you're right. We're pretending to be CIA. And there's a bomb we need to defuse, and if we don't get out of here soon, our team is going to lose and then we have to drink a gallon of milk without puking."

"Aw, that sucks. I gotcha, man. Come on, let's find your teammate. But, Zeke?"

"Yeah?" I said.

"Next time, ask me to play too. Sounds like fun."

"I will. Now come on."

We ran through the sewers, water splashing up all around us, soaking my pants. I didn't have time to think about how soggy and chilly I was. We needed to find Sparrow.

Then I heard a sound.

"Stop," I said. Kyle halted in his tracks. I heard it again. It sounded like *eek.*

It was Sparrow.

"Sparr—I mean, Stephanie!" I shouted. I began to jog toward where I thought the sound was coming from. The light wasn't very good down there, so I had to follow the shadows.

We rounded several corners, doubled back twice, and then came upon Sparrow. She'd hit a dead end.

"There you are," I said. "Come on, we need to—"

"Just lead me to the way out," she said, her eyes steely and dangerous.

"Wow, Stephanie doesn't mess around," Kyle said.

"You have no idea," I replied. "Okay, let's all stick together. The exit is this way."

I'd memorized all our various routes, and after ten minutes of slogging through the muck I found the ladder that led back to the surface.

"You first," I said to Kyle.

"Got it."

My friend clambered up the rusty ladder, pushed open the grate above, and disappeared. Sparrow went next. Once there was enough room, I went last.

My heart was beating like a hummingbird. We had to

figure out how to stop Le Carré. I trusted that Sparrow would know what to do once we'd all reconvened outside.

Instead, what I saw once I climbed through the grate chilled me to the bone.

Standing inside the shed was the massive, evil Ragnarok. In the crook of one massive arm he was holding both Kyle and Sparrow by their necks. They twitched in the grasp of his huge white gloves, the only thing keeping them from being burned alive by his molten skin. Kyle was petrified, his eyes bugging out of their sockets. Sparrow was struggling, but the huge monster's arm was the size of her entire body.

Ragnarok's red, red eyes focused on me. He'd fixed his visor. Red streams of magma flowed through his custom tubing. For a moment, I marveled at the science of it all, the physiology. What a creature this…thing…was.

And then Ragnarok spoke.

"I have no use for this one," the monster said, squeezing Kyle's neck harder. My friend's face was going blue.

"He can't breathe!" I screamed. "Let him go!"

"I have no use for him," Ragnarok said. "He will live. But you two *parasites* must die."

With that, Ragnarok threw Kyle to the ground. He didn't move. Then the monster grabbed Sparrow by the neck. I ran at him and tried to rip at the magma tubing. I couldn't even scratch it.

"Let her go!" I yelled. "Take me! That's what you all wanted, right? The codes? I have them!"

The monster let loose a deep, bellowing laugh. His red face turned a shade of crimson. I could have sworn I saw a red tear drip down his cheek.

"I know who you are, Zeke Bartholomew. I hope your friend thanks you for what you've gotten him into."

Ragnarok reached back, and his massive paw was suddenly around my neck. I struggled. He squeezed. I couldn't breathe, couldn't draw air into my lungs. I was fading…and so was Sparrow.

Spots appeared in front of my eyes. Then, just as I was about to lose consciousness, Ragnarok lifted us both off the ground and one at a time dropped us back into the dark, dank sewer.

I landed on my back, pain shooting through my legs. Sparrow landed next to me. I heard a terrible thud. She screamed and held her arm. Her shoulder looked out of place, and she rolled on the ground, clutching it.

I ignored the pain, gathered myself, and ran to the base of the ladder. I looked up.

Ragnarok was holding Kyle again. My friend was still breathing. Something to be thankful for.

But Ragnarok had removed the glove from his right hand. In that glowing appendage he held a small black orb. He squeezed it, opened his hand, and I saw that the orb was glowing a bright, shining red. Smoke cascaded from it.

My eyes widened. He was holding a fire grenade.

"Move!" I yelled to Sparrow. Grabbing her around the waist, I threw us forward, just as the beast tossed the red, smoking grenade into the sewer.

There was a huge explosion, and then everything went away.

SEWAGE TREATMENT

3:47 p.m.

Four hours and thirteen minutes until everything goes Kablooey and I'll never get an iPad.

I don't know how long I was out for. It couldn't have been too long, because when I came to I couldn't breathe.

My face was underwater. I lurched up, spat water out of my mouth, coughed, and snorted it out my nose. It was terribly dark, and I couldn't make out much of anything except the acrid smell of smoke from the fire grenade. Ragnarok had been waiting for us.

He'd needed to know where we were. He needed to know we weren't coming after him.

He had Kyle.

I felt an awful pang in my gut when I realized that the

sick, molten monster had taken my best friend. And my only hope was…

Sparrow?

"Sparrow!" I shouted at the top of my lungs.

I couldn't see her, couldn't see anything, really, so I felt about in the dark. Feeling for something, anything, that would let me know where she was.

"Sparrow!" I shouted again. "Where are you?"

I tripped over a rock. A pile of them actually. I went down in a heap and bashed my elbow.

I rolled over, holding it and rocking back and forth. I'd ruined everything. I shouldn't be here. I shouldn't have put my family and friends in danger. And now here I was, sitting alone in the bottom of a destroyed sewer system. My best friend was kidnapped, and the girl who'd saved my life had disappeared.

Then I heard a noise.

Eek.

Eek.

Kids in grade school used to call me that. It started one Halloween night. A kid named Steve Berg (Isabel Berg's brother) had lost both of his front teeth. He tried to call me "Zeke," but it came out "Eek." That stuck for far, far too long.

Eek.

"I hear you, Sparrow! Where are you?"

"Here," came the voice.

I followed the noise to where it seemed to be coming from.

"Speak again!" I said. "I'll follow your voice."

"I'm over here," she said. There wasn't much energy in her voice. I had to find Sparrow.

I followed the voice for a minute before I came upon her. My heart sank.

"Oh, no…Sparrow…"

She was lying on the ground, cradling her arm. I remembered that sickening sound when she'd hit the floor. Noticing the angle she was holding it at, I could tell that her shoulder was definitely separated.

But more worrisome was that her entire lower body was buried under rocks. Some big ones. I couldn't even see her legs.

"I tried to pick them up, get them off me," she said lethargically, "but I couldn't with this." She gingerly moved her damaged wing.

"Don't move," I said. "I'll do it."

I stepped forward and began to remove the rocks from

Sparrow's fallen body. Some of them were quite heavy, so I concentrated on the smaller ones first. I began to see clothes, skin. Her uniform was tattered and shredded. There was blood on her legs.

"I'll get you out of here," I said. "I'm not leaving."

Once I'd taken the smaller rocks off of her, I started on the larger ones. I couldn't move them on my own. There was a small crack of light that illuminated the hallway just enough for me to go scavenging. I found a sheared-off pipe and used it for leverage.

I propped the pipe under the larger rocks, then pushed down, propelling the rocks off of Sparrow's body. One at a time. I had to be careful. I didn't want a rock to fall back on her.

Once most of the rocks were gone, Sparrow was able to push a few of the smaller ones from her. Finally she was free. I knelt down and leaned in close.

"Are you…okay?" I asked.

Sparrow stood up. She wobbled for a moment, placing her good hand on my shoulder to steady herself.

"I'm so sorry," I said. "I should have known."

"Stop whining, you little baby," Sparrow said. "Now, help me."

"Help you what?"

"Get my shoulder back into place."

"Uh...how exactly do I do that?"

"Just follow my instructions."

"Okay..."

Sparrow cleaned off a space in the corridor, then lay herself flat on the dirty ground. She took several deep breaths, steadying herself. Then she clutched her elbow to her side and slowly began to raise her arm, almost like a bird's wing. She gritted her teeth, small sounds escaping her lips.

When her arm was at shoulder level, she said, "Now you come in."

"What do I do?"

"Help me move my hand behind my head. Like I'm trying to scratch my neck."

I knelt down and gripped Sparrow's hand and arm gently. My heart was beating fast. I slowly began to rotate her arm ninety degrees. When her hand got behind her head, she let out a small yelp. I nearly fell backward.

"Come on, there's no way this is more painful for you than for me."

"Yesterday I was forgetting to do my calc homework.

Today I just got firebombed and I'm sitting in a pile of rubble playing orthopedist. Forgive me if I'm not a robot."

"Come on, C-3PO. Keep going."

I moved her arm until her hand was behind her head.

"Okay, now what?"

She replied, "Now pull my hand straight, in the direction of my other shoulder. Do it right, and it should pop the joint back into place."

"What if I do it wrong?"

"Then you'll probably shred every ligament in my shoulder."

"Great. No pressure."

Gently, I began to pull her hand. It was difficult, and her arm was already at an odd angle. Sparrow was sweating, biting her lip. It must have taken every ounce of effort not to scream.

"Keep going," she breathed.

"It won't go any farther," I said.

"Yes, it will. That's the point. On the count of three, pull my hand as hard as you can."

"I don't think I can."

"One," she said.

"Wait, let's talk about this..."

"Two," she continued.

"I'm not that strong."

"Three!"

On "three" I yanked her hand. There was an awful popping sound, and Sparrow shrieked. She rolled onto her side as I lurched backward into a puddle.

"I'm so sorry!" I said. "I didn't know what I was doing! Are you okay?"

Slowly Sparrow rolled over and got to her knees. She was still clutching her arm. Bracing herself on the wall, she stood up. Gently, she let go of her cradled arm. It hung limp at her side.

Then she began to move it. Rotating, swiveling, raising. She was still clearly in pain, but…

"The joint is back in place."

"Okay good, because I was this close to yakking," I said.

"The ligaments have been pulled and stretched, but it's back."

"Good."

"Now we need to get the heck out of here, find Ragnarok and Le Carré, and stop SirEebro before it brainwashes every kid on the planet."

"So you're okay?" I asked, amazed that someone who'd

just been buried under hundreds of pounds of rubble could still be such a pain in the butt.

"I'm fine," she said. I pointed at her arm. "Not bad. Won't need surgery. Long as I can take the pain, it won't hold me back. And, yes, before you ask, I *can* take the pain."

"I wasn't going to ask," I said. "Okay, yes, I was."

"Is there any way we could get back up through the entrance?"

"No way," I said. "Ragnarok blew the ladder to smithereens. No way we can climb back up."

"What about the other doors down here? Any chance we could get through them?"

"Far as I know, they're all locked. The only one that isn't is...the GeekDen. Come on!"

The GeekDen might have been far enough away from the blast that it might still be standing. I cautiously stepped through the destroyed brick and rubble, finding my way through the sewers to our hideout. The whole tunnel looked like a bomb had hit it. Ragnarok wasn't kidding with those fire grenades. It was a miracle we were still alive.

"It's up there," I said. "It's right over...here. Oh, no."

The door to the GeekDen had been blown in. It was in three pieces. And inside, all of my gadgets, all of my hard work, it looked like someone had, well, thrown a fire grenade inside.

"My stuff," I said. I went around the bombed-out room, surveying the damage. There was not a single item that hadn't been affected in the blast. My vegetable grinder-upper. Vaporized. I'd invented it as a kid when I didn't want to shovel broccoli into my mouth. You simply inserted a vegetable into it, and it ground the produce into a powder so fine that it could be sprinkled on the rug undetected, for either a vacuum cleaner or family pet to Hoover up.

My automatic textbook reader. For the days when my eyes were just too tired to read thousand-page textbooks. I invented the device to place on a given page, and a robotic voice would read the chapter to you. Saved me from getting Coke-bottle glasses by the age of eight.

And my proudest invention, the HoloZeke. Using light refractions, mirrors, and video footage, once installed in my room it gave off the illusion that I was sitting at my desk, studying, when in fact I was elsewhere, likely in the GeekDen, inventing more amazing gadgets. I always left my bedroom door open a crack so that my dad could peek in, see the HoloZeke, and think I was studying. But in reality I was in another world.

My world. And now that world was destroyed.

"Everything I worked so hard on," I said, surveying the destruction. I felt like someone had ripped out my heart, spat on it, and laughed at it. I turned to Sparrow. The look on her face was pure apathy.

She shrugged.

"Doesn't matter anyway. It was mostly junk."

"Junk?" I said, shouting. "This was my life's work!"

"And now it's a pile of trash," she said. "And we're stuck in here."

I couldn't even speak, I was so mad. How could she not understand? How could she be so cold?

"Listen, Zeke, I get that you're upset. But the fact is, we wouldn't be in this mess if not for your little den of geeks or whatever. You can sit here and cry over frayed wires. I'm going to figure out how to get us out of here."

"Right. Just like you figured out how to fix your broken ComLet. Oh, right, sorry. That was *me*."

"You'll make a great DVD repairman someday," Sparrow said. "See you on the outside."

She walked away, cradling her injured arm.

There was no way Sparrow was getting us out of here. Not with a recently dislocated shoulder, and not without the ComLet to signal for help. By the time the police came, Le Carré's plan could be under way and Kyle might be dead. I couldn't listen to Sparrow. She was like everyone else in my life. Telling me only what I couldn't do. It was time to show her what I *could* do.

I stepped into the wreckage that was my old lab. Bits and pieces of metal and wood were everywhere. I had to look at it unemotionally. What was in here? What could I use?

There. In the corner. It was still intact…

And there, under a broken table…a few of those might do the trick…

And that puddle in the corner. It wasn't water, it was a spilled bottle of…

I ran around the lab, gathering bits of shredded and blown-up things, and put them all into the center of the room. I bit my lip. I had no idea if my idea would work, but it was our only chance.

For the next fifteen minutes I gently assembled it. Some things you learned from spy movies; other things you learned as you went. I'd never tried to make one, and would never suggest anyone else do it either. But desperate times call for geeky measures. And when it was finished, and swishing around in the old Drano gallon container I found, I carried it out into the sewer.

There I found Sparrow. She was standing by a wall of rocks, her arm at her side, her good limb trying to pry out some of the massive rocks to create a tunnel.

At this rate, she'd have us out of here by the time teleportation beams were invented.

"Here. Let me try," I said.

She turned around. First, I had something to show her.

"Here," I said, handing her a piece of wood wrapped in twine.

"What is that?" she said.

"A splint. For your arm."

I could tell she didn't want to accept it, but she didn't have much of a choice. I helped her, gritting my teeth as she winced, and strapped the splint to her arm. She sighed.

"A bit better. Thanks."

"Now for the hard part. Move aside so I can take a look at this."

"I'm doing fine," she said, defiantly.

"Listen, Sparrow, or whatever the heck your real name is since you're all secretive and shady and all that. It doesn't mean anything right now. You're hurt. And I can get us out of here. So you can play the 'I'm an emotionless spy and I can do anything and blah blah blah' game, or we can try to save the world and my best friend."

She stepped back. "Okay, Brainiac. What do you suggest?"

I held up the jug.

She furrowed her brow. "You're going to use Drano to get us out? You're more hopeless than I thought."

"After all we've been through, I'd have thought you'd give me a little more credit."

"Nope," she said.

"Okay, fine. You don't have to give me anything. But you're going to want to get far, far away from here?"

"Um…why?" she asked cautiously.

"Because I'm going to blow a hole in this wall."

"You're going to…you made a…a…"

"A bomb. That's right. And it's going to save our behinds."

"You made a bomb in your blown-to-smithereens GeekDen?"

I smiled inwardly at her referring to it by its proper name.

"That's right. Who deserves some credit now?"

"Is it going to work?"

"If it doesn't, I hope you have laser beams in your eyes, because I'm out of ideas. Now, get back. *Way* back."

Sparrow turned and jogged to the sewer junction.

"Farther," I shouted. "At least a hundred yards."

I heard the patter of Sparrow's feet in the water as she went farther back. I felt around the broken wall. There was one spot that seemed to be relatively less dense than the rest. I set the jug down and threaded a piece of wiring into the cap. Then I took out the pack of matches I'd saved from the GeekDen and opened it. Just two matches. Of course.

I pulled out the first one and struck it. Nothing. I struck it again. Still nothing. Flustered, I struck it again with such force that it sparked up, and immediately went out.

Crap.

I was sweating. One match left.

I took it out. Held it. Stared at it.

"Come on, little match," I said. "You're our only hope."

I held the match against the matchbook and struck it

and...the match leaped out of my hand and landed in a puddle of water.

"No," I said, scrambling to pick it up. The head was soaked. It was useless. "No. Nonononononono..."

It was over. We'd have to wait. I'd failed. I'd come so close, only to let Le Carré win. I let down Sparrow. Kyle. My father. Everyone. Because I was too clumsy to light a match.

I knelt down. Tried not to cry. Then I felt a warmth on my hand.

A small ray of light, illuminating my knuckles. It was coming through the demolished wall. A small speck of sun was sneaking through.

I looked around. This wasn't over yet. I went back into the GeekDen and picked up a shattered magnifying glass lens. Then I angled the lens so that it reflected the sunlight onto the fuse.

The fuse began to simmer. Then it began to smoke. And then, just like that, it burst into flame.

I'd done it! I lit the fuse!

Holy crap, that was one short fuse!

I turned around and sprinted as fast as my unathletic legs would carry me. I could hear the fuse burning behind me. I had five seconds, ten at most. I reached the junction, and just as I was about to turn, just as I saw Sparrow crouching behind a boulder, a massive eruption threw me off my feet, sending me sprawling.

I hit something hard and felt a pain shoot through my shoulder. Then I was all wet.

I couldn't move. My body ached. I smelled smoke. I tried to sit up. Then I felt an arm wrap around my waist.

"Come on, Zeke." It was Sparrow. She was using her good arm to help me up.

I got to my feet, steadied myself.

The corridor was filled with thick smoke. We coughed and approached the wall. Suddenly the smoke lifted and lightened. Through the haze I could see a hole in the rocks, no more than two feet high and a foot and a half wide.

But outside there were trees.

"You did it," Sparrow said. "Now, come on!"

She ran toward the hole, letting me drop into the muck. I sat there, regaining my breath, smiling. When it returned, I got up and jogged forward, ready to save the day.

DAYLIGHT IS OVERRATED

5:02 p.m.

Two hours and fifty-eight minutes until I never get to eat my dad's spaghetti and meatballs again. On the plus side, I'll never have to eat his Mandatory Monday Meatloaf again either.

It took my eyes a minute to adjust to the sun. It wasn't as bright as I would have thought, which meant the day was slowly slipping away. Which meant Le Carré's plan was coming closer and closer to fruition.

Sparrow was standing just a few yards ahead of me, rubbing her shoulder. I jogged up to meet her.

"Where is Le Carré's hideout?" I asked her. She turned to me but said nothing. "Don't you know?" I said. "Don't the people at SNURP know?"

She replied briskly. "Don't you think if we knew

where he was, we would have shut his whole operation down by now?"

"Well, that's just spiffy," I said. "What do we do now?"

"The ComLet is no use. So I can't radio for help. We need another way of figuring out where he's headquartered."

I saw a tree stump nearby. I walked over to it and sat down.

"What do you think you're doing?" Sparrow shouted at me.

"I'm thinking," I said.

"We don't have time for you to pick your nose."

"First off, you could be a little nicer to me, considering I got us out of that hole. And second, it's not like I'm slowing down some plan. We've lost our leads. Ragnarok is gone with Kyle. We don't know where Le Carré is. We don't—"

"We don't what?" Sparrow said.

"Maybe we do."

Sparrow came over to where I was sitting.

"Spill it."

"Derek Lance moved in next door to me, and the car that picked me up was full of Le Carré's men. If this plan is scheduled to go off today, there's no way they would have wasted time driving, unless..."

"Unless Le Carré's headquarters was within driving distance."

"Exactly," I said. "Now, let's think about SirEebro. That kind of machinery doesn't run on triple-A batteries. It would require an enormous power source. Something far beyond what this town has. It has to be something that would register. Something that would show up on a thermogram."

Then it hit me. How we could find Le Carré.

"Come on," I said. "Can you run?"

"Can I run?" she asked quizzically.

"With your arm like that."

"Faster than you can."

"That's what I thought you'd say. Come on, there's not much time."

I took off running, and heard Sparrow matching me stride for stride. I wasn't in the greatest of shape, and it didn't help that Sparrow had the constitution of an Olympic sprinter. I began to pant and sweat and huff, and even with a damaged shoulder she looked to be exerting as much physical energy as I did when sharpening a pencil.

It was just about a mile away. The houses and trees and roads all began to look familiar. I had reservations about going there, but we didn't have a choice. I just hoped he wouldn't be...

"Zeke!" my dad cried out. He was standing in our driveway. I used a bad word under my breath.

We ran up to the driveway, where my dad gathered me up in his arms and squeezed me harder than I'd ever been squeezed in my life. Not counting the giant Ragnarok, but for different reasons.

"Where have you been?" he said. His face was unshaven, eyes red, and he looked like he hadn't slept a wink. "Nobody's been able to find you, you haven't answered your cell phone. Are you all right?"

"I'm fine, Dad. Let's go inside. I'll explain everything."

"Of course, right..." He looked at Sparrow. "Who is—"

"I'll explain inside."

We followed him into the house. He poured us each a glass of water, and we downed it in seconds. And a second and third glass. My dad sat at the counter, waiting expectantly, dying to know what happened.

"Okay, here's the story," I said, not sure what my next sentence was going to be. I couldn't tell him about Ragnarok, or SirEebro, or Le Carré. Not that he'd believe me anyway. "We've been...this is...I—"

"I'm his girlfriend. Wendy."

We both looked at Sparrow. Both our jaws were hanging open.

"You're his…"

"You're my…" We spoke at the same time.

Sparrow walked over to my dad and extended her hand. He shook it, wearing a look on his face like he'd just been told he'd won a contest to go live in an ivory tower with a troupe of goblins.

"Wendy Peters."

"Wendy," my dad said, trying to process everything. "You're Zeke's…"

"Girlfriend," she repeated. "It's new. Right, honeybunny?"

I choked on my water.

"Right, Zeke?"

"Right. Of course, um, sugarbear."

"We were out playing flag football and got so exhausted that we just fell asleep on the field. Sorry we weren't able to call."

"Right," I said. "And I forgot to take my phone out of my pocket, and it broke during the game."

"You were playing…football?" my dad asked. He couldn't have been more surprised if I'd told him I'd been practicing hang gliding.

"Just flag football," Sparrow said. She touched her shoulder. "Banged up my shoulder a little bit."

"Yeah...shoulder..." my dad said. I could tell that half of him wanted to be relieved I was home, half of him angry that I hadn't gotten in touch, and half confused beyond belief. But that was three halves. Which made as much sense as anything did right now.

"Anyway, Dad, we can talk more later, but Wanda and I—"

"I thought her name was Wendy," he said.

"That's what I said. Wendy."

"You said 'Wanda.'"

"You're hearing things, Dad. Anyway, we need to go over a problem set that's due tomorrow. Can we talk later?"

"Right. Later. I need to see if we have any beer."

As my dad went to the fridge, I led Sparrow upstairs to my room. Once we were inside, I shut the door and locked it.

"'Sugarbear'?" she said.

"Like it's any worse than 'honeybunny.' Obviously you've never actually had a boyfriend, because the only people who call themselves honeybunny and sugarbear are, like, lame old people."

"Why are we here?" Sparrow asked.

I looked around my room. Ordinarily I would have been mortified to have a stranger, let alone someone like Sparrow, in my room, but I didn't have time to freak out. The world was at stake. And the only thing that could save it was one of the very first inventions I'd ever created. Only it hadn't quite been created for the task at hand.

I pulled out a trunk from under my bed. There were numerous locks on it. Sparrow shook her head.

"What are you keeping in there, the mystery of Atlantis?"

"Ha-ha. Ha-ha. And I'm totally not being sarcastic. This is how we're going to find Le Carré."

I opened the mass of locks—combination 4-8-15-16-23-42—and opened the trunk. It revealed dozens and dozens of gadgets of varying shapes and sizes. From a pen that never ran out of ink to my old movement detector. But what I was searching for was at the bottom.

I pulled out what looked like a metal rod attached to

a small LCD monitor. Wires and batteries ran along the sides, and the whole thing was held together by duct tape.

Sparrow looked at it like I'd just sneezed in her face.

"That's going to save the world?"

"I'd think I've earned a little trust so far."

"Okay, Brainiac. Explain."

"A few years ago," I said, "Kyle and I heard that some kids from our grade were starting a bonfire, making s'mores, all the good stuff. But we didn't hear about it until later that night when we got an accidental text message from Donna Okin. Obviously someone forgot to tell us, so we had to find it ourselves. So I built this. I call my own personal thermography device. I call it the 'HeatSeeker Four Thousand.'"

"Why Four Thousand?"

"I dunno. It sounded cool."

"Go on."

"The HeatSeeker Four Thousand can find large sources of heat within any given radius. Now, the larger radius you set it to, the more juice is needed to power it. Hence all the batteries. If I can find a few more batteries, we can find the largest sources of heat within a thousand-mile radius. And I have enough batteries lying around here that it should do the job."

"How…how did you make this?"

I couldn't be totally sure, but Sparrow sounded moderately impressed.

"It's actually similar in theme to a common thermometer. Everything generates heat. Vehicles, even people and animals. Using a combination of mercury and electric power, I can use the HeatSeeker Four Thousand to find things that emit large amounts of heat. It shows up on the LED screen. Yellow denotes smaller sources of heat. Red, larger. The redder, the hotter."

"So we're looking for something that would emit enough heat to power SirEebro."

"Yes. Red, big-time."

"What ended up happening with the bonfire? Did you find it?"

I paused for a moment. Bad memories.

"Yeah," I said. "We found it."

"And?"

"When we got there, the kids just started laughing. Turns out we weren't supposed to have been invited at all."

I waited for Sparrow to offer a sympathetic word, but

she didn't. There was a small twitch in her eye, but that was it.

"Anyway, I think this can help us. Look around for extra batteries. Anything. Just start pulling them out of remote controls, toys, anything."

Within minutes, we'd pried batteries from my cordless phone, my Nintendo DS, a penlight, my portable computer speakers, even a remote-control car that had somehow found its way under my bed and that I hadn't seen in years.

I hooked them all up to the HeatSeeker 4000 and turned it on. The LCD popped on. Sparrow and I huddled over it. Several red dots began to appear on the screen. Some were faint; some were a harsher red, indicating larger sources of power.

But still, nothing of the magnitude that would have been needed to operate SirEebro.

"Where is it?" Sparrow asked.

"It's not on the screen."

"I can see that. What's wrong with your gizmo?"

"Nothing's wrong with my 'gizmo,'" I said, letting my annoyance show. "It's obviously outside the range we have enough power for."

"So we need—"

"More batteries," I said.

"There aren't any more. We emptied your room."

"I know." I put my hand on Sparrow's uninjured shoulder. "I need you to go distract my dad."

"Excuse me?"

"I need to go into the living room. He's got, like, seventeen remote controls there. Ask him to give you a tour around the house or something."

"I...I can't do that," she said.

I cocked my head. "You dive-bombed me from the sky. You survived a fire-controlled monster and a homemade bomb. You're telling me you can't engage my dad in small talk?"

She looked at me like I'd asked her to translate ancient Greek into Sanskrit.

"You know? Small talk?"

Now she was figuring out how to turn the Sanskrit into pig Latin.

"Just ask him normal things. To show you around. What his job is like. Baby pictures of me. Scratch that, there are some of me naked in the bathtub. Just anything!"

"I—"

"Suck it up, spy. Get down there and engage my father in small talk!"

Sparrow hesitantly stood up. She looked at me, then at the door, then back at me. I thrust my finger toward the door.

She walked toward it, opened it, and went down the stairs. Slowly.

I crept to the top of the stairs and listened.

"Hi…um…Zeke's dad," she said tentatively.

"Oh, hey, there, Wendy!" my dad replied. "How are you two doing?"

"We are doing just peachykins."

Peachykins? Had she never spoken to someone's parents before? I banged my head against the banister.

"Are you hungry? Thirsty? We have some diet soda and tomato juice."

"No. That's all right. My thirst doesn't need to be quenched."

This was getting painful. *Get to the point, Sparrow,* I thought.

"I was wondering, Mr. Bartholomew, father of Zeke. Do you have any pictures of Zeke naked in the bath?"

Thankfully my lungs stayed inside my body, because I almost coughed them out.

"Um...yeah, I think so. You want to see photo albums?"

"Affirmative."

"All right, then. Don't tell Zeke I'm showing you these. He'd stop speaking to me for a week."

"I will not tell Ezekiel."

Okay, I had to concentrate before my head exploded. I heard footsteps as my father led Sparrow into the den, where he kept all of our old photo albums. I hadn't looked through them in years. I always had a hard time with it. Mom was in them. Easier to keep them closed. Not to think about it.

I crept down the stairs. A pair of French doors separated the den from the rest of the house. We rarely closed them, only if we were watching a particularly cool action movie where we wanted to feel like we were closed off in our own theater. That's where dad had introduced me to James Bond. Simon Templar. Indiana Jones. Great memories that shaped me into the dork I am today. Sparrow and my dad were sitting on the couch with a large photo album splayed open between them.

"That's Zeke after he threw up an entire can of SpaghettiOs," my dad said.

I cringed. Dad and I were going to have to have a long talk, assuming I made it through the day alive.

As they were facing the opposite direction, I gently closed the French door, squinting, waiting for a telltale creak that would give me away. Thankfully the doors closed without a sound. I allowed myself to breathe. Stealthily, like a ninja.

Then, when I turned around, my elbow knocked a small vase off a shelf, which fell to the floor and shattered into a thousand tiny, ornate pieces.

"Zeke?" my dad shouted from inside the room. "Everything okay out there?"

"Yeah!" I shouted. Just dropped an…ice cube tray."

"Pick it up, will you? Don't want it to melt and warp the floor."

"No problem!" I shouted back.

I ran into the kitchen, took the small dustpan and broom from the closet, swept up the pieces, and tossed them into a garbage bag. No harm, no foul. My dad wouldn't even notice it was gone. Oh, who was I kidding? He'd want to have a serious talk with me too. Assuming I made it through the day alive.

I went into the kitchen. Out came the batteries from the flashlight my dad kept under the sink. Out came the batteries from the cordless phone. I felt a little bad about that one. Grandma Betty called every night at eight o'clock. She would have to stick to email for a while.

I pillaged all the remote controls and electronic devices I could find and carried the batteries up to my room. Then I pulled out my roll of duct tape and set to sticking the whole contraption together. It wasn't easy; if one battery moved and disconnected it would disrupt the entire circuit. It took the whole roll of tape to get it all together and immobile.

When it was done, I went back downstairs and knocked on the door, just as I heard my dad say, "This is Zeke after a bird pooped on his head."

Yes, he had taken a picture of it. My dad. Always classy.

"Um, guys?" I said, opening the door gently.

My dad looked up and smiled.

"Hey, bud, just showing Wendy here some of your greatest hits."

I wasn't sure that "bird poop" and "greatest hits" belonged in the same thought, but there was no time to argue.

"Wendy, isn't it close to dinnertime? Don't your parents want you home?"

"Oh, right," Sparrow said, pretending to look at her nonexistent watch. She stood up and extended her hand to my dad. He wasn't sure what to do with it. Not many twelve-year-old girls were so formal.

He took her hand, shook it.

"It was a pleasure to meet you, Mr. Bartholomew," she said.

"It was nice to meet you too. Don't let Zeke show you his comic book collection," he said with a grin.

My hand was beginning to hurt from all the mental slaps I was giving my dad.

Then, after they finished shaking hands, Sparrow curtsied. I snorted a laugh, unable to contain it.

"So proper!" he said. "You could learn some manners from Wendy, Zeke."

"Right. I'll be sure to curtsy for Mr. Statler tomorrow. Come on, Wendy, I'll walk you home."

"Oh, you live in the neighborhood?" my dad asked. "Where's your house?"

Sparrow looked at me, her eyes wide with panic.

"She, uh, her family is moving. Let's go. Just let me grab my wallet," I said.

"Bye, Wendy!" my dad called out as we ascended the stairs.

Once upstairs, I grabbed my backpack and threw the

HeatSeeker 4000 inside, along with a few other gadgets I thought might come in handy. It was a bulky contraption. I carefully carried the backpack downstairs and we left the house.

"Now what?" she said.

"Now let's see if our Duracell family picks up on Le Carré's hideout."

Once in the driveway, I took the gadget out of my bag and turned it on. It grew warm in my hands. I hoped it wasn't frying my brain as I held it.

Red dots began to appear all over the screen. Small images, nothing too powerful.

"There's nothing there," Sparrow said.

"Hold on," I said. "Let me zoom out."

I enlarged the search radius. Then, at the top of the screen, I noticed something.

It was very faint, but there. A smidge of red at the very top of the screen.

"See that?" I said to Sparrow.

"Looks like nothing. It's faint."

"I'm not looking at the brightness; I'm looking at the width. It's at least three or four times wider than any other dot on the screen."

"What does that mean?"

"It means there's something big out there."

"Okay, so where is it?"

"I…I don't know. This is zoomed out as far as it goes. It's a fifty-mile radius. So it's somewhere within fifty miles of here."

"Well, we're not going to find it by walking or taking the subway. How do we search within that radius?"

I looked around. I had no idea how we were supposed to travel.

Then my eyes fixated on the house next door. The Lance home. There were two cars in the driveway. I figured the family owed me one.

"Can you unlock and hot-wire a car?" I asked.

"Can you eat soggy cereal for breakfast?" she replied.

"Yes, I can."

"Then let's go."

We crept over to the Lance driveway. There were still security cameras everywhere, but we didn't have time to worry about them. I kept watch on the house as Sparrow sneaked up beside the sedan, and within seconds she was inside without having triggered the alarm.

Then she ducked her head under the steering column.

"Hurry up!" I whispered loudly.

She shot me a look. I shut up.

Thirty seconds later I heard the car rumble to life.

"Get in!" she shouted from behind the wheel.

I didn't hesitate. I sprinted over, jumped into the passenger seat, and seconds later we had hightailed it out of the driveway and out onto the road.

I held the HeatSeeker 4000 in front of me.

"Head north by northwest," I said. "And do it fast."

"You've got it."

She sped out onto the highway.

"Don't go too much over the speed limit. Last thing we need is to get pulled over right now. Two underage kids driving a speeding stolen car won't look too good. My dad will think I'm a bad influence on you."

Sparrow kept it at an even seventy as we sped along. Slowly but surely, the hazy red smudge at the top of the screen grew brighter, more distinct.

"That's gotta be it," I said. "I've never seen anything come out that bright. It's got to be an incredible power source."

"How long till we get there?" Sparrow asked.

"Not sure. All we can do is keep going, using this as our compass."

And just as luck would have it, the moment I said that, the HeatSeeker 4000 shut off.

"Oh, crap," I said.

"What happened?"

"It died," I said.

"What the heck was the use of getting all those batteries?" she said. "And where should I go?"

"Just keep going straight. I can fix this."

I rummaged around in my backpack and pulled out another GeekDen contraption. I pulled the plug out of the cigarette lighter and threw it in the backseat. Then I hooked a device into the socket and attached it to my battery circuit.

A second later the HeatSeeker came back on, the dots brighter than ever.

"Nice work," she said.

"Never thought I'd be using it for this," I said. "Okay, start veering more west."

She followed my directions. Soon the smudge was fully visible. And it was impossibly bright.

"It's gotta be within about ten miles. This thing is hot. Keep going."

Sparrow sped up. I was about to tell her to slow down,

but then I saw the clock on the car dashboard. If our information was accurate, Operation Songbird was going to take effect within the hour. There was no time to lose. The fate of the world was in the hands of a kid who was once selected after a mop for a kickball team. (The gym teacher wouldn't let that stand—though he did get a laugh out of it.)

I had a hard time arguing that one. At the time.

I watched as the huge red orb grew agonizingly closer. Sparrow kept looking over to the HeatSeeker 4000 to see as well.

"We're getting close," I said. She just nodded.

We had driven outside of the town limits, the highway passing numerous small strip malls and roadside diners. There were no signs of a super-villain hideout. Not that it would have exactly advertised itself. You wouldn't be a successful villain if you had a lair in the shape of a huge, evil trident, or surrounded your castle with a moat filled with floating dead bodies. Le Carré's crib was hidden. It made sense that it wasn't visible to the naked eye.

"Turn off at the next exit," I told Sparrow. She complied.

We drove off the exit ramp and headed west until we were right smack in the middle of the red blob.

I looked back at the HeatSeeker 4000.

"Something's wrong," I said.

"What?" Sparrow asked.

"We should be here. I don't understand."

"Then where is it?" she asked.

"I…I don't know. Stop the car."

Sparrow pulled over to the side of the road. On one side was a forest. On the other side was a strip mall.

"I don't see anything," she said.

"Me either." I looked toward the forest. Then the strip mall. Then at the device. The red blob was large enough that the radius was at least a mile in any direction. Which meant we could spend hours combing through leaves or wandering sidewalks and still find nothing.

"Zeke," Sparrow said. I snapped to attention. Her eyes showed something I hadn't seen before: fear. We were running out of time and Sparrow knew it.

I had a vision in my head of Stefan Holt, seventh-grade newsman, standing in front of a camera with one of those wireless microphones in his hand.

Reporting live from the scene, where the world has been

overrun by übervillain Le Carré. The streets are in chaos, and nothing will ever be the same again. I'm standing here with Ezekiel Bartholomew, the only person who had a chance to stop Le Carré and rescue his best friend, the gangly Kyle Quint. Zeke, what does it feel like to have failed miserably and let down millions of people?

I felt like I was going to throw up. And this time I didn't need ipecac.

There had to be something we'd missed. Le Carré was around here somewhere.

I scanned the trees. The roads. The strip mall. Looking for something, anything out of the ordinary.

"Zeke," Sparrow said, a hitch in her voice. "What now..."

"Wait," I said. "There."

I spotted something. I took a few steps closer to make sure. Squinted. There was no reason for it to be there. I knew right then that I'd found Le Carré.

"What is it?" she asked.

"That coffee shop," I said. "Look at it."

"It looks like a coffee shop. I don't think a venti macchiato is what we're looking for."

"No, not *at* the stop, *above* it."

Sparrow moved closer. "Is that—?"

"An FTM Twenty/Four mobile. Commonly used by the military to set up communications."

"Why the heck would there be a mobile military antenna above a coffee shop?"

"There's no reason for it to be there," I said, "unless there's something inside that requires the kind of communications network that needs military operating power. Universal telecommunications power. The kind of power that—"

"Could broadcast all over the world," Sparrow said with horror.

"Exactly," I replied. "We found him."

I DON'T EVEN LIKE COFFEE

6:51 p.m.

One hour and nine minutes until a bunch of zombie kids with the IQs of a cucumber march all over the world. (Did Sparrow really pretend to be my *girlfriend*? Sorry, still shaking my head at that one. I mean, who does that? Wait, where was I...oh, yeah, the world's about to end. Priorities.)

When I was ten, I sneaked a swig of my dad's morning roast. I nearly threw up. It made my head swim and my heart beat what seemed like a thousand beats per minute. I knew coffee was a stimulant, but I had no idea it would make my heart feel like the Road Runner was galloping full speed inside my chest. I hate coffee. Hate the smell, hate the taste, hate the weird variations that people have come up with, hate coffee shops and bars, and even the word *barista*.

So naturally it made sense that Le Carré would use a coffee shop to disguise his base. Like I needed any more reasons to hate him.

I pulled my laptop out from my backpack and plugged in the wireless card. I ran a few quick searches and found that the shop had been purchased by new owners three years ago. The company name it was registered under?

"Ragnarok Industries," I said.

"You've got to be kidding me," Sparrow said.

"Come on," I said, stepping out of the car and hitching the backpack over my shoulder. "We need to find out what's really going on in there."

We jogged over to the coffee shop, threw open the door, and walked inside. Immediately the smell of ground beans and milk infused my nostrils and made me gag. And gag again.

"You okay?" Sparrow said.

"Yeah, it's just," I said, hiccuping, "the smell of coffee makes me nauseous."

"Wonderful. Is there anything that doesn't turn you into Jell-O?"

I threw her an evil glance.

We looked around the shop. About a dozen people

were sitting at tables, sipping coffee, munching on pastries, or buried in their computers. Three baristas worked behind the counter, looking as excited to be there as I always was during my yearly physical.

Nothing looked out of the ordinary. It was a coffee shop. They served real coffee. If Le Carré wasn't here, I was going to be mighty peeved for putting my nostrils through this kind of agony.

"Let's take a look around," I said.

"Will do," said Sparrow.

I walked around the left side of the café; Sparrow took the right. I eyeballed the people sitting down, trying to see if they looked shady, if maybe they were working on some top-secret project having to do with world domination.

"Hey, kid, stop staring. You're creeping me out."

I snapped out of it, realizing I'd been staring at one guy's computer while he perused what looked to be an online dating site.

"Everyone does it these days. Get a life. Go away."

I obliged Mr. Hard Luck in Love and kept walking.

I walked around back. More tables, more coffee, more people. There was nothing here.

I knelt down and started to look underneath the tables, trying to see if there were any secret buttons, strange panels, or floorboards that could be pried up.

I felt a tap on my shoulder.

"Excuse me, sir?"

I stood up. "Yes?"

One of the baristas stood over me. He was a youngish guy with hideous chin hair that looked like the result of a particularly gruesome weed whacker experiment and enough facial rings and piercings to make getting through an airport metal detector a daylong activity.

"Some of the patrons have been complaining that you seem to be, um, peeping at them. Their words, not mine. I'm going to have to ask you to stop or to leave."

"I'll stop," I said. "Sorry. I'm looking for my dad, who's supposed to be meeting me here. He's late again as usual."

I put on my best "poor me" face and the enemy of all metal detectors backed off.

"Oh, hey, listen, no problem. Take your time. Hope your dad gets here soon."

"Thanks," I said, wiping an imaginary tear from my cheek.

Once he was gone, I did another lap and headed over to

meet Sparrow. I couldn't find her. I went around to the right side of the café and saw her standing in front of an elevator door.

"Hey, what are you doing?" I asked.

"Ever seen an elevator in a coffee shop before?" she said.

"No, but it could lead to a storage room."

"No, the storage room is in the back. I saw one of these scary-looking bearded people bringing bags of beans from there. And there's a delivery door in the back as well. There's no reason for this to be here."

I scratched my lip. She was right. There was something down there. But it still didn't fully add up. I just didn't picture Ragnarok—in his flame-retardant suit and jetpack, carrying my friend Kyle—waltzing into a coffee shop and calmly pressing the Down button.

"There's got to be another entrance," I said. "Something that leads below. Just not in the shop. I was stupid. It's below us, but the real entrance wouldn't be so public. It'd be somewhere hidden. Somewhere in the thick of things. Somewhere..."

Suddenly I turned around and sprinted outside.

"Zeke!" Sparrow yelled, chasing after me. "Where are you going?"

I didn't have time to explain. She was a faster runner than me anyway, so I knew she'd keep up.

I zoomed through the parking lot, waited until traffic parted, and ran across two highway lanes until I reached the thick forest on the other side. Only twenty yards in and you could barely see the cars, and they sure couldn't see me. Another twenty yards and you wouldn't even know civilization was on the other side.

I stopped to catch my breath. My heart was pounding, and not just because I wasn't in very good shape.

"Zeke," Sparrow said, pulling up next to me. Naturally she was totally cool while I was practically bent over, panting. "What are we doing?"

"Hold on."

I looked around. For something. Anything. If I didn't find it soon, that Stefan Holt report would become a reality and something very, very bad would happen, even worse than the time I'd studied for an entire day's worth of wrong tests.

Then I found it. Not by sight, but by smell.

"You smell that?" I asked.

"Smell what?" Sparrow replied.

"A faint odor. Hydrogen peroxide. Just a trace."

Sparrow took a whiff of the air. "I smell something. What makes you think it's a lead?"

I turned to her. "Ragnarok was wearing a jetpack. Jetpacks, or their first iterations, were invented by the Germans during World War Two. In nineteen fifty-nine, two American scientists attempted to harness the technology. They realized that the best fuel to use for jetpack propulsion was—"

"Hydrogen peroxide," Sparrow replied.

"A hydrogen peroxide–based substance, yes. Ragnarok was here," I said. "He landed somewhere around here. Let's follow the scent."

We spent ten minutes trying to triangulate the location of the hydrogen peroxide smell. Not too easy, considering there was a faint breeze that made pinpointing it darn near impossible. Then I heard…

"Zeke!" It was Sparrow. I jogged over to where she was standing. And I saw why she'd called me over.

The smell was strong, but more important was a circular patch of grass on the ground, about four feet in diameter.

It was completely singed.

"He landed here," Sparrow said.

I knelt down. There were matted imprints in the grass, a large boot print. It was definitely him.

We followed the boot prints until they stopped...right before a massive oak tree.

I walked up to the tree. Inspected it. It was huge, with branches filled with leafy green leaves spindling out in all different directions.

"This one," Sparrow said. "Notice anything?"

I looked closer. At the very base of the branch was a very faint demarcation line.

"This branch has been sawed off and then put back on," I said.

"Or," Sparrow said, "it's not a branch at all."

"Heck, it works in the movies. Here goes nothing."

I reached forward, took the branch with both of my hands, and pulled.

The branch rotated in my hands. Smoothly, like it was on gears.

I nearly fell back. It continued to rotate even though I'd let go of my grip.

And as the branch turned, a panel in the wood slid open, revealing a shiny, gleaming metallic pod.

I heaved a breath, realizing I'd forgotten to exhale for nearly a minute. Sparrow turned to me, and I said, "Let's go save the world."

I GET MICROWAVED

7:09 p.m.

Fifty-one minutes until some guy with a funny accent in his name destroys everything. And is his first name really Le? His parents must have wanted him to get made fun of more than mine.

We walked into the capsule, and the moment our feet crossed the threshold, the fake wooden door whooshed shut and suddenly we were hurtling downward at a speed far faster than any normal elevator.

"I think I'm going to be sick," I said.

"For once in your life can you go thirty seconds without threatening to puke?"

"Um, not today."

"Fine."

Sparrow looked around the capsule while I did my best

to keep my lunch where lunches are supposed to stay.

"I don't see a camera," she said.

"Me either," I replied.

"That's not a good thing. It means somebody definitely knows we're coming. And wherever we're going, we're going there fast, which means when we get there, we're going to have a welcoming party."

"Okay, so what do we do?"

"Go over by the wall," she said.

"Okay." I did as she told me.

"Now give me a boost."

"Okay. Um, what?"

"I can push out one of these ceiling panels," she said, pointing. "We need to get on top of the elevator."

"Um...why?"

"If there are no cameras, they know that whoever is in this elevator isn't supposed to be here. But since there are no cameras, they don't know who we are. We need to get out of sight. Now, boost me up."

I knelt down, cupped my hands, and held strong as Sparrow put her boot into the hold. On the count of three, I lifted her with all of my meager might until she was able to reach the ceiling.

She slipped her finger inside her uniform and pulled out a small file. Using it, she began to unscrew a ceiling panel. As she was doing so, the elevator began to slow down. We were nearing the bottom.

"Hurry," I whispered.

"Going as fast as I can."

One screw came out. Then a second. Then a third. One left. The elevator was slowing down even more.

"Done!" she said as the fourth and final screw fell to the floor. There was a loud scraping sound as Sparrow pushed the ceiling panel away, revealing hundreds of feet of empty blackness above us.

"Push me up."

I did, and she clambered through the hole and into the elevator shaft. Then she leaned back down, the wind whipping her hair about her. She leaned over and stuck her hand down.

"Grab it, and I'll pull you up."

I reached up and took her hand, and she began to pull. I could hear her grunting in pain, the shoulder she'd separated not making things any easier.

"Stop!" I shouted, letting go of her hand and falling back to the floor.

"What are you doing, Zeke? We're almost there!"

I bent down and picked up something from the floor. The fourth screw that she'd loosened from the ceiling panel.

"Don't need anyone finding this," I said. She smiled.

"Now, come on."

I gripped her hand, and at the same time she pulled, I reached up and was able to get my other hand through the hole and onto the top of the elevator. She pulled, I pushed, and soon I was sitting next to Sparrow on top of the elevator as we descended through the darkness.

I looked up. I couldn't even see the entrance we'd come through. No wonder Le Carré's headquarters couldn't be found. It was thousands of feet below the ground. That's what the mobile military antenna across the street was for. There was no way he could get the necessary reception down here, no way he could broadcast with SirEebro without a mechanism on the surface to do it.

I helped Sparrow replace the ceiling panel, and we sat and waited as the elevator continued on its downward path. There was a small grate through which I could peek down and see the inside of the empty elevator.

"Odds are they'll just inspect the elevator and leave. Then we can go about finding and destroying SirEebro," I said.

Sparrow nodded.

The elevator slowed down, slowed down, and finally came to a grinding halt. I did the quick math. I estimated that we were at least a mile below ground. Unfathomable.

"A quick check," I mumbled, "and then—"

Suddenly the air erupted in huge thunderbolts. We covered our ears as sparks and smoke blew up in the elevator right below us. Red beams of light blinded me. The shock waves sent us both tumbling off the top of the elevator. I was able to grab a cable to hold on to, preventing myself from falling over the side to my death. I couldn't see Sparrow but couldn't risk calling out to her. Not that she could have heard me anyway. It was like the Fourth of July times a thousand less than five feet away from us.

Finally the explosions stopped. I was afraid to breathe. Quick inspection, my butt. They opened fire without even waiting for the doors to open. I'd been five feet from being Swiss Zeke.

"All clear," said a male voice from below us.

"Elevator is secure," a female voice said.

"Must have been an electronics malfunction. Send a repair team."

That's odd, I thought. Those voices sounded strangely familiar…

I could hear footsteps in the elevator, which went away after a few seconds. When it appeared that we were alone again, I hoisted myself back on top of the elevator, trembling like a little bird. Sparrow was above me, clutching a cable. She slid back down and joined me on the elevator top. We both looked down.

"Wow," I said. "I think they even shot up all the dust particles in there."

"What were those things they were firing?" Sparrow asked.

"It didn't sound like gunfire," I said. "And those beams were some sort of laser rifle. I've never seen or heard of anything like it before."

"Let's admire their handiwork later," Sparrow said. "Coast is clear. No time to waste. Let's move."

She began to remove the ceiling panel again, but I grabbed her arm.

"Are you nuts? There could be a hundred guards just inside waiting for us. We go down there, I'm half the kid I used to be."

"So what do you suggest?" Sparrow asked.

I pointed across from us to an open air vent.

"There," I said. "We make like tunnel rats."

She looked below, then looked at the burned-to-smithereens elevator below us. My option seemed like the choice least likely to get us pureed.

"Okay. You first."

"So ladylike," I said. "Come on."

There was no way I could squeeze through the vent with my backpack strapped across me, so I tied it to my ankle. I slid across the top of the elevator and barely pulled myself through the air vent. I could feel the fat on my love handles squeaking as I shimmied through the vent. The backpack slid behind me, thankfully not making much of a sound.

"Maybe cut down on the waffles for breakfast," Sparrow said.

"Right. Because I balance my diet based on how many evil air ducts I'm going to have to crawl through on a given day."

I kept going. There were noises below us, but I couldn't make anything out. Still, something stuck in the back of my mind. I recognized those voices back in the elevator.

The man and woman who'd blown it to kingdom come. I had no idea how or why, but something told me I knew who was down there with Le Carré. Nevertheless, I had to find Kyle.

We came to a T-junction, splitting off to the left and the right. Both trails curved off, preventing us from seeing where they led.

"You go left, I'll go right," Sparrow said. "But neither of us does anything without letting the other know what's down there. We meet back at this junction in five minutes."

"You got it," I said, trying to sound brave, but in truth ready to soil my underwear at the prospect of skulking around a secret, guarded underground lair without Sparrow. Still, she was right. It was the only way to know for sure; a few wrong turns and we would run out of time.

I began to shimmy left while Sparrow went right. I crawled along the corridor, nothing but metal surrounding me on all sides. My backpack was still attached to my ankle, and I pulled it along with me as I moved.

I could still hear voices below me, and my breath caught in my throat every time my fat made a noise that might give away my position.

After about fifty yards, I came to the end of my line. The vent was sealed off by an air duct. I shimmied to the very end and saw that the vent was about fifteen feet off the floor. What I saw below me made me nearly cry out.

It was Kyle.

He was sitting in a cell, beams of red light crisscrossing the entrance. His head was in his hands, and he was nibbling on his fingernails. A common Kyle trait when he was nervous.

I could see spots of blood on his hands. He'd chewed through his nails and was now eating his cuticles. Gross.

Every few seconds Kyle would raise his head up to look at something outside his cell that I couldn't see. He looked tired, scared, hopeless. I wanted to reach out to him, to let him know that Zeke Bartholomew was here to save the day.

Actually, I'm not so sure that would have made him feel any better.

I waited until a little while had gone by without any movement from Kyle—which meant he wasn't being watched at the moment—and then reached into my pocket and took out that last screw Sparrow had dropped in the elevator. I aimed carefully and tossed it into Kyle's cell.

It pinged at his feet, startling Kyle, who leaped up.

"Sit back down!" a voice outside the cell shouted. Kyle did as the voice ordered.

But then he reached down and picked up the screw. Turned it over in his fingers. Then, slowly, he looked up. And based on the totally incredulous look in his eyes, I knew he saw me.

Kyle's jaw dropped.

I waved at him. Because, well, I didn't know what else to do.

I motioned for him to stay put. Kyle's mouth flapped open and closed. I couldn't rescue him right now. The air duct was too high for him to climb up to, and there was no sense in my dropping down into a guarded cell.

So, as much as I hated to do it, I mouthed to Kyle, *I'll be back*.

His eyes basically said, *You've got to be kidding me. Get down here and get me out of here!* And his mouth let loose a silent barrage of obscenities that I'm pretty sure he hadn't learned from Mrs. Hooverville, our English teacher. I don't even think the majority of them *were* in English.

Hopefully he'd understand in a little while.

I tentatively turned around, trying to make as little noise as possible, and began the shimmy back to the T-junction to meet Sparrow.

A few minutes later I arrived back just in time to see her coming around the bend. She met me in the middle.

"Did you find anything?" she whispered.

"I found Kyle. They're holding him in a cell at the other end of that tunnel. Some sort of infrared laser gate, same color of red as those beams inside the elevator. I can't get him out from here. We're going to have to find another way. What did you find?"

"I think I found another way," Sparrow said. "That tunnel leads to a generator room. I didn't see anyone inside. We can go from there."

"Good. Because I told Kyle I'd be back."

She cocked her head. "What do you mean you told him you'd be back?"

"Well, I didn't *tell* him, tell him. I threw a screw at him, and I think he saw me and got the picture."

"So you're telling me that he clearly acknowledged you."

"Yes."

"The prisoner that they're guarding and probably have cameras on at all times."

"Yes."

"You're telling me he looked directly at where you were lying."

"Yes, why are you…oh, no…"

The second my stupidity registered, the metal enclosure around us erupted in a cascade of sparks and fire. Red laser beams cut through every inch of the metal tubing, miraculously missing us by millimeters at most.

I screamed. Who wouldn't? Laser holes poked every inch around us, cutting through the metal like it was paper.

"Come on!" Sparrow yelled.

I crawled behind her, covering my head, but trying to avoid the lasers in a small, enclosed tube was like trying to avoid getting wet in the shower. I felt them slice through my clothes, felt them singe my eyebrows.

We tried to make it to Sparrow's side of the tunnel, but then there was an awful lurching sensation, and the entire duct system around us broke free, fell through the air, and down to the ground.

The wind was knocked out of me, and the smell of smoke and gunfire made my dad's barbecue seem appetizing. I coughed and hacked and tried to open my eyes through the dust.

Then, finally, I opened my eyes. And what I saw in front of me made my head spin. I knew why I had recognized those voices from before.

Standing over us, with strange-looking rifles pointed directly in our faces, was the singing duo of Penny Bowers and Jimmy Peppers.

LE CARRÉ HAS TERRIBLE TASTE IN MUSIC

7:34 p.m.

Twenty-six minutes until...whoa, that's less than half the time of my afternoon algebra class. I'm starting to get kind of worried here...

"I hate your music," I said to the two pop singing sensations, who, for reasons that boggled my mind, were aiming battery-powered laser rifles directly at my brain. My dad had always told me I use only half of my brain sometimes. Jimmy and Penny looked like they were ready to get rid of the unused half.

The two singers didn't flinch. Hey, they'd probably heard that before, likely in much harsher language.

Just as surprising as the fact that these two crooners were here was that they were both wearing their trademarked

Penny Bowers and Jimmy Peppers outfits. Bubble gum to the max. Kids around the world bought their merchandise with more enthusiasm than if it were a guide to tomorrow's homework. Why were these kids here, and why were they wearing their outfits? They just didn't seem all that conducive to terrorist activities. Not that I was the terrorist fashion police or anything.

"Stand up," said Jimmy.

"Both of you," said Penny.

"Wow, even when threatening to kill people, you two are in perfect sync," I said.

We stood up. I untied my backpack from my ankle. It was immediately confiscated by Jimmy. As if I needed any more reasons to dislike him.

I had to admire their firepower. The rifle barrels were long and sleek, and there appeared to be a battery charger attached at the base that powered the lasers. There were five green light panels running atop the rifle, but only three of them were lit. I noticed Jimmy flick a switch, and two more panels went dark.

Interesting.

My guess was that each gun had five panels worth of power. The more light panels were on, the more powerful the blast. As if confirming my thoughts, Penny switched the power on hers from three to one. My guess was that three-panel blasts were what had torn up the elevator and air ducts. One panel was probably enough to kill. I shuddered to think how powerful a five-panel blast might be.

Pretty cool technology. If you wanted to take over the world. Or destroy it.

"Penny and Jimmy," Sparrow said. "These are those singers you were telling me about."

"That's right. They're responsible for rotting billions of brain cells around the world."

"Stop talking," Jimmy said.

"Both of you," Penny added.

"It's like you share the same brain," I said.

"March," Jimmy said, prodding me in the back with the barrel of his gun.

"You too," Penny said, doing the same to Sparrow.

"Okay, you're really starting to freak me out," I said.

They pushed us forward. We were in a large, open space with ceilings about twenty feet high, metallic walls, and what felt like a titanium floor. It was incredibly hot down here. I imagined we had to be near the reactor that my HeatSeeker 4000 had picked up.

"He wants to meet you," Jimmy said.

"He's very impressed by you," Penny added.

"'He' wouldn't happen to have a sandwich, would he?" I said. "Because my stomach is ready to eat itself."

They pushed us forward toward a closed doorway. Jimmy pulled the gun from my back and went to go type in a security code.

"Zeke?" Sparrow said.

"Yeah?" I replied.

"Silence," Penny said.

"Quiet," Jimmy added.

"Duck!" Sparrow yelled.

I did so immediately, and suddenly there was a whirlwind of action behind me. I heard a bunch of *thunks* and *pows*, and suddenly both Jimmy and Penny were on the ground.

"Run!" Sparrow yelled.

I reached down and yanked my backpack from Jimmy's grasp and then followed Sparrow's sprint back the way we came.

We ran by the wreckage of the air duct and through an open door at the other end of the chamber.

The room was filled with dozens of pumping pistons and gears, and it was hotter than my dad is when I come home from school after having forgotten to do last night's geometry homework.

There was one particularly massive machine in the center of the room, surrounded by a metal railing. I looked down. The railing was guarding against a hole so deep and vast I couldn't see the bottom.

"This is it," I said. "This is the reactor. This is what's powering SirEebro."

"We need to find a way out. We need to destroy SirEebro."

We sprinted around the outside of the room, looking for something, anything, a way to get free. There was nothing. No rooms. No doors. Only the huge pit underneath the main reactor.

We were trapped.

"Sparrow," I said, "what do we do?"

"I don't—"

Before she could answer, I heard a noise above us. I looked up just in time to see an enormous shape come crashing down onto the floor right in front of the reactor.

It was Ragnarok. And he looked mighty peeved.

I turned to run, but a nanosecond later five huge fingers were around my throat, literally lifting me off the ground. I couldn't breathe. All the blood was draining out of me.

Gack was the only sound I could muster.

"Come out," the massive molten giant said, "or I snap your friend's neck like a twig."

Sparrow's head peeked around the corner. Her eyes went wide when she saw us. I couldn't get free. I mouthed one word to Sparrow.

Run.

She was the only one who could save the world. I had to sacrifice myself for her.

She shook her head, stepped out of the shadows, and walked directly up to the immense man. She looked up at him, blinked, then hawked up a big loogie and spat it directly onto his visor.

Ragnarok smiled. He placed my feet on the ground, but his fingers were still wrapped around my windpipe. They loosened just enough to allow air into my lungs.

Then his other hand shot out and grabbed Sparrow by the neck, and he began dragging us back toward the other room.

"I told you to run," I gasped out.

"I'm not leaving you," Sparrow said, wriggling in the giant's grasp.

I didn't know what to say. I would have done the same for her. But I didn't know what good it would do everybody else who was at risk.

Ragnarok dragged us through the other room. To my surprise, Jimmy and Penny were gone. Guess Sparrow hadn't knocked them totally out.

Still holding my neck, he used one finger to press several keys on a code pad. The door in front of us opened, and he took us into one of the most incredible rooms I've ever seen in my life.

There was a mammoth screen in front of us that had to be at least fifty feet high and a hundred feet across. Various antennae and projectors were stationed all around the perimeter. Video screens lined the walls, showcasing live scenes from around the globe. China. India. Brazil. Australia. Africa. London. Dozens of desks and modules littered the floor. And in front of the enormous screen was a large cube with blinking lights and dials and wires that looked light-years beyond anything I could have ever dreamed of making.

"SirEebro," I said.

There was a whoosh of air, and the cube opened in front of us. The two halves separated, revealing a man sitting inside. He stood up. Turned around. And walked toward us.

He was bald, completely hairless, and held a cane in his right hand. He wore a purple outfit, skintight, with black seams crisscrossing his body. His nose was hook sharp, and a thin beard ran from his sideburns down his jaw, over his lip, and under his chin. And there was a small, furry animal perched on his shoulder. It had beady eyes and sharp teeth and seemed to like me as much as its master.

He walked right up to us and nodded at Ragnarok.

"Mr. Bartholomew. Ms. Sparrow. I am Le Carré. And this here is Higgins."

"Higgins?" I said. "What is he?"

"Mr. Higgins is a marmot," Le Carré answered.

"Hey there, little Higgins!" I said, approaching the oversized rodent. Higgins gnashed his teeth, and I leaped back a split second before my fingers ended up in his fuzzy belly.

"Really, Zeke?" Sparrow said.

"Sorry. He looked friendly."

Le Carré pressed a button on his lapel and said, "Bring in Mr. Quint."

Seconds later another door opened, and Kyle was

brought through. At his back were Penny Bowers and Jimmy Peppers, holding rifles. I was really, really starting to hate those two kids.

"Zeke!" Kyle said when he saw me. He ran forward and gave me a monster hug. Funny, since my throat was still in Ragnarok's clutches.

"Kyle," I choked out. "I can't breathe."

He let go. Then Kyle kicked me in the shin.

"That's for leaving before."

I cried out in pain but couldn't even bend over to rub my ankle.

"I said I'd be back!" I told him.

"Zeke," Kyle said. "What the heck is going on? Where are we?"

"You are about to witness one of the greatest moments in the history of mankind," Le Carré said. "Throughout the ages, tyrants have come and gone. Men have tried to bend the masses to their will, only to fall short. I will succeed where they have failed."

Ragnarok let go of Sparrow and me, and I took a moment to catch my breath. I had a feeling those massive paw prints would leave a mark. If I ever made it out of there alive, people would ask what I had been doing being mauled by a gorilla.

"This device, SirEebro, is about to broadcast the most powerful message in the history of civilization," Le Carré said.

"I don't know. I've heard their music. Personally, I think dog poop is slightly more important."

Le Carré laughed. He didn't seem fazed by the insult. Nor did he seem like the kind of person who listened to Top 40 radio.

"As you know, the message isn't the music. It's what's behind the music."

"I think I saw that special on MTV at three in the morning."

"I'm glad you can still laugh," Le Carré said. "I can assure you that in about ten minutes the only person who will be laughing is me, and I'll be laughing for a very long time."

"I have one question," I said.

"Please. Your questions are inconsequential at this time."

"So we figured out your plan. You're going to use SirEebro to broadcast a hidden signal within the new PB&J single that will zombify everyone who hears it. Hundreds of millions of people will be under your control."

"Amazing, isn't it?" Le Carré said.

"Yeah, although 'amazing' is not the word that first comes to mind. But Penny and Jimmy are booked on every television show from the moment the single airs. Each show will rebroadcast the music. Anyone who misses the debut will still be brainwashed."

"That's the idea. And you're underestimating, Ezekiel. Billions will be under my control."

"Right. Billions. But if they're supposed to be on live television in just a few minutes...what the heck are they doing here?"

Le Carré thumbed his lip. Penny and Jimmy kept their laser rifles trained on us, one green panel lit on each gun.

"I suppose it can't harm you to know the truth," he said. Le Carré pressed another button, and an image came on-screen. I gasped when I saw it. It was a live feed from what looked like the dressing room at a talk show. There was a food platter, water bottles, and a famous talk show host I recognized sitting on a couch.

And sitting next to him, laughing like they'd just heard the world's funniest joke...were Jimmy Peppers and Penny Bowers.

"How..." Sparrow said, "how is that possible?"

Le Carré pressed one more button. A door on the far side of the room slid open. And if my jaw could have hit my shoes, it would have, because suddenly dozens of Jimmy Peppers and Penny Bowerses marched into the room, each of them carrying their own laser rifle.

"You've gotta be kidding me," I said.

The lined up in front of Le Carré, at least ten rows, at least a hundred of them.

"Penny Bowers and Jimmy Peppers are robots?" I asked, dumbfounded.

"State of the art, manufactured under my specific plans. Once the message goes out, millions and billions of people will follow these robots to take over every piece of our world. Media. Government. Television. The Internet. People will follow Penny and Jimmy to the end of the earth and bring about its end until I am supreme master of all that remains."

"You're a sick, twisted man," Sparrow said.

"History is made by such men," Le Carré said. "The future is claimed by men like me."

Ragnarok stood there, and darned if I didn't see a smile under that freaky visor of his.

"In ten minutes the broadcast will go out, and my army

will be there to lead. Nothing can stop them. Nothing can stop me. And you will be witnesses."

"You're forgetting something," I said.

"Oh? Is that so?" Le Carré asked, amused.

"When your goons picked me up, they needed the access codes to SirEebro from SNURP. Without those codes, SirEebro is just a tin can. You can't broadcast without those codes."

Le Carré put his hand to his head and feigned being stunned. "Oh, my dear boy, you're right. How will I ever be able to broadcast without those codes that my men foolishly thought you possessed?"

"That's what I'm asking, you tyrannical doofus."

"It's because *I* have the codes, Mr. Bartholomew."

"How? You couldn't have gotten them in such a short amount of time," Sparrow replied angrily.

"You've forgotten the key to my whole plan," he said.

Sparrow spat, "And what key is that?"

Suddenly another voice said, "Me."

We both turned around. My blood ran cold. I knew that voice.

Standing next to Ragnarok, as though he'd appeared out of nowhere, was Derek Lance.

SUNGLASSES IN THE DARKEST NIGHT

7:51 p.m.

Okay, you get the picture. We're running out of time. I always liked these ticking clock things in movies, but I feel like my heart is about to explode. Why did I agree to do this again? Maybe it would be more fun to be a brainwashed zombie kid. Like, I'd never care about homework again. Then again, I'd never care about anything again. Even my dad. Okay, bad idea, let's try and stop these creeps. We've only got nine minutes to save the world...

You," I said.

"Hello, Sparrow," Derek said, stepping forward and embracing her. She wriggled out of his grasp. "Come on, don't be like that. You and I got along so well in training. Now you don't want to say hello?"

He was wearing an impeccable dark suit, a red tie, and his mirrored sunglasses hid his evil eyes. For a diabolical madman, Derek Lance sure could dress.

"We got along before I knew you were a coward and a traitor who sold your soul to the devil," she said.

"My soul is pretty much intact, but this sale did increase my bank account substantially," Derek said. He winked at Le Carré, who smiled. "Now, babe, we have front-row seats to the beginning of the end, and a new beginning. Why don't you come here, sit on my lap, and we'll watch together. Like we used to."

I looked at Sparrow. "You and him?"

"My first girlfriend," Derek said. "You don't get to meet too many girls when you're a spy. Thankfully Sparrow and I were training at SNURP at the same time. I think she'd admit I helped her through some tough times. Did she tell you her real name? It's—"

"Say one more word," Sparrow said, her eyes gleaming with fire, "and I will come wring your neck, and I don't care what happens next."

"Don't worry, sweetie, your secret is safe with me." Derek looked at me. "My former classmate. Zeke Bartholomew. The amateur."

"This amateur found you out, you, you, bombastic simpleton."

"Wow, even your insults are amateur hour. Listen, Zeke, I'm kinda impressed that you stayed alive this long. Doesn't reflect well on this big lug right here." Derek shot Ragnarok a disapproving glance. The monster just glowered, as most monsters do.

"Don't get a big head, my friend," Derek continued. "Every dog gets lucky from time to time. Most kids, they're just as stupid as you. They'll follow anyone anywhere. They already follow Penny and Jimmy like they're saviors. Well, all my main man Le Carré is going to do is show the world how right I am."

"My army of children will be unstoppable," Le Carré said. "Millions swarming east and west. A tidal wave of small soldiers."

"And you're going to let this happen," Sparrow said.

"Let it happen?" Derek said, laughing, his tie fluttering ever so slightly. "Baby, I'm *making* it happen."

"You're lucky I don't kick those sunglasses down your throat."

"If you even tried," Derek said, "I'd kill you so fast I wouldn't even need to take my suit jacket off."

"It's a cheap jacket anyway," I said.

Derek cocked his head. "This suit is worth more than your house."

"Too bad the guy wearing it isn't worth the crud I clean out of the gutters."

Derek stepped forward to me. He took his sunglasses off. His eyes were a piercing blue.

"I have half a mind to kill you right now," he said.

"Go ahead," I replied. "Why wait? What, you'd rather these freak-show dolls or this molten mutant did it? Let them. At least I'll know it wasn't at your hands."

Derek looked at Le Carré. The mastermind did not move.

"All you are is an errand boy," I said. "You delivered a message. How brave."

"Shut up," Derek said.

"Or what? You'll go find codes that will make me be quiet. Go ahead, big man, show me what you've got."

Derek marched over to one of the Jimmy Peppers robots and pulled the laser rifle from its hand.

I circled slightly to my left.

Derek walked back and stood directly in front of me. I could tell by the way he held it, he'd never used that type of rifle before.

The gun currently had one green panel lit. Enough to kill me. But not enough for what I had in mind.

Le Carré said, "In five minutes they'll be dead anyway. You can wait, Derek."

"Yeah, Derek," Sparrow chimed in. "You can wait."

"I don't wait for anyone," he said, thumbing a button on the side of the rifle. A second green light flared up.

"You're a patsy," I said. "A nothing. That rifle isn't going to do anything more than give me an electric shock. You don't even know how to work it."

"Derek..." Le Carré said, walking toward us.

"I do too," he said, and thumbed the rifle button three more times, lighting up all five panels.

I looked at Sparrow. She gave me a slight nod. We were on the same page. This was it. The moment it all came down to. The fate of the world was in the hands of a kid who had once let a dodgeball bounce off of his head three times before hitting the floor.

"Then go ahead and shoot, Lance, or are you nothing but an empty suit?"

At that split second, Sparrow charged up from behind Derek Lance and threw her entire body weight into him, just as he pressed the trigger on the laser rifle.

A massive red beam exploded out from the barrel, Sparrow's weight caused the laser to divert from its intended target, instead cleaving a hole right through SirEebro. The metal box erupted into flames, the sides melting down where the laser had perforated it.

Le Carré let out an anguished howl as steel and sparks rained down around us.

The blow had knocked the gun from Derek's hand. I sprinted over, dove, and picked it up. And just as I did, I felt a massive hand close around my neck.

Ragnarok. And this time he wasn't going to just hold me tightly.

I could feel his huge fingers digging into my windpipe. I did the only thing I could. I aimed the rifle up in his direction and pressed the trigger.

Another pulse emanated from the rifle, and suddenly I was free. I looked at the monster. A faint wisp of smoke was coming from the floor next to him. The blast had cut right through a molten lava tube on Ragnarok's arm, and he was literally leaking thousand-degree liquid onto the floor. He howled in agony.

I turned back to the room and yelled to Kyle and Sparrow, "Run!"

Then I fired one more blast at the Penny and Jimmy army. A dozen robots exploded as the rifle torched them.

As we ran out of SirEebro's chamber, I heard Le Carré yell, "Kill them all!"

We ran through the next room as I fired blasts behind me without looking. There were enough huge explosions and raining debris for me to realize that SirEebro was officially out of commission. Le Carré wouldn't be able to broadcast the PB&J single to the world. Sparrow and I had just saved millions of lives.

How we were going to get out without losing our own lives was something I hadn't quite figured out yet.

"Go for the elevator!" Sparrow yelled.

"It's destroyed!" I answered.

"We're not going to use the actual elevator," she said.

I gulped.

The three of us ran as fast as we could, Kyle ahead of us, his long legs much quicker than ours.

"There it is!" Sparrow shouted. Less than twenty yards away were the burnt remains of the elevator we'd come down on. Sparrow and Kyle pried the doors open, Sparrow wincing with her injured shoulder.

Then I felt something plow into me from behind, and I went sprawling. I turned to see Derek Lance. His fist cocked back and then, before I had a chance to move, landed just below my left eye. A burst of pain exploded in my head, and I went tumbling backward.

My head smacked on something metallic and hard. It was the railing in the reactor room. Had I lost my balance, I would have fallen to my death.

The lair was falling apart. We had only minutes, if not seconds, before the whole thing collapsed with us inside.

"I'm going to kill you, amateur hour," Derek said, his hands closing around my throat. I was getting a little tired of that. I moved my head back, swung it forward, and head-butted Derek Lance right in the cranium. He stumbled back and we both tumbled to the ground.

Then, from the corner of my eye, I saw something coming. It was Ragnarok. He was leaking molten lava, leaving steaming puddles as he moved. He was weak, the burning life draining out of him. And he was coming right for us.

Just as the monster was about to crash into both of us and send us all plummeting thousands of feet to our doom, I pulled Derek down to Ragnarok's knee level. The unbalanced monster tripped over our prone bodies and, unable to stop himself, flipped over the metal railing and crashed into the reactor. Several of the lava tubes crossing his body were cut, and magma spurted everywhere. I felt a drop of it graze my arm, like a hot poker. Then the monster fell noiselessly into the abyss.

Derek and I stood there for a moment in shock. We looked at the reactor. Lava had begun to eat through the metal, smoke pouring from dozens of tiny holes.

That was not good.

I heard footsteps. Many of them. The PB&J army was coming for us.

I pressed Derek up against the railing, but he wouldn't budge. And his hands found my throat again.

"You'll die now," he said, teeth gritted into a maniacal snarl.

"Hey, Lance," I said, with all the air I could muster. "Nice shades."

I drew my hand back, and with all my might I thrust my index finger right through his sunglasses and into his eye.

Derek staggered back, holding his face. I could see blood dripping between his fingers.

I turned and ran. Sparrow was fending off the PB&J army with the rifle, but they were beginning to return fire.

"Come on!" Kyle yelled.

We piled into the broken elevator, and one by one clambered on top of it. The three of us stood there, fire snaking out into the elevator shaft. In mere seconds the reactor would overheat and we'd all be dead.

Sparrow gripped the elevator cable. "Hold on, guys," she said.

"Are you crazy?" I said.

"Only the crazy survive," she said.

Kyle and I grabbed the cable and held on for dear life. Sparrow aimed the rifle down at the elevator, at the opposite cable, and pulled the trigger.

The blast illuminated the elevator shaft in a brilliant red light. The elevator exploded, and the cable across from us snapped in half.

Then we were zipping through the air, being whisked upward at speeds my dad would never let me drive at in a million years. I could feel my hair and my lips being pulled back. I'm pretty sure I was screaming, but I couldn't hear a thing.

Suddenly a huge fireball erupted directly below us and began chasing us up the elevator shaft. It was gaining on us.

I looked up. I could see the top of the shaft. We were almost there. But I didn't know if we could outrun the fireball.

A hundred yards. Fifty. Thirty. Twenty. Ten.

The cables hit the roof of the shaft at full speed, rattling our bones with the huge jolt. Kyle and I managed to hold on, but I heard a cry of pain and saw Sparrow's shoulder give out. She was going to fall directly into the fiery pit. Holding on to the elevator cable with one hand, I caught her good arm with my other.

Kyle reached down and grabbed it too. We pulled until Sparrow was back with us, then the three of swung onto the ledge where we'd entered the elevator not too long before. We pried our fingers into the small slot between the doors and pulled it open.

Then we all squeezed through the small opening until we fell into a heap back in the woods outside. We were safe.

"Keep running!" Sparrow shouted as she jumped up. Soon she was ten yards ahead of us.

She'd been right so far, so Kyle and I stood up and began to run. And we kept running.

Then, behind us, the entire woods seemed to explode into a massive fiery ball, right where we'd stood just seconds before.

We kept running until we got to the strip mall with the coffee shop. The military antenna had melted onto the roof of the shop. The woods were burning. The reactor had exploded. The PB&J army was now destroyed. Le Carré and his plan had been defeated.

We'd won.

I rolled over, coughing amid all the smoke and ruin. I saw Kyle lying on the ground a few feet away. I crawled over and shook my friend.

"Kyle!" I said, slapping him in the face. "Kyle! Speak to me!"

"Ugh, stop slapping me, you turdburger."

He rolled over. Aside from being covered in ash and looking like he'd just slept for a week in a fireplace, he appeared unhurt.

"Zeke," he said, "right now I'm just happy to be alive, but at some point real soon you're going to have to explain to me what the heck just happened."

"I will," I said. "I will."

I stood up and looked around, but I couldn't see her.

"Sparrow!" I shouted. I ran back and forth, checking under logs and broken branches. "Sparrow! Where are you?"

I spun around, looking for some sign of her. Anything.

But Sparrow was gone.

I'VE NEVER BEEN THE CAMPING TYPE

8:17 p.m.

Seventeen minutes since we saved the world. I think...

"This is Stefan Holt, reporting live from the scene of the crime. What we have here is an explosion of the highest magnitude, with fire and brimstone raining down all across the horizon. What has happened here we do not know for certain yet. Hey, Dad, can I have a hot chocolate?"

Okay, so Stefan Holt wasn't *really* reporting live from the scene, but his dad was, and the kid kept pretending to report his own fake newscast while peppering his working dad with annoying questions, such as whether they could go across the street and get snacks from the coffee shop sitting atop a molten lava reactor cave.

I watched Stefan Holt's dad report the real news.

Rumors were they had to break into other breaking news: that the new PB&J single had debuted to critical panning. Kids around the world hated it. The duo had canceled all appearances and concerts for the indefinite future. And according to their publicist, both would be taking a step back from the spotlight, perhaps permanently.

We got to see some of the publicist's press conference on a closed-circuit TV in the back of one of the news vans. I recognized the publicist immediately: it was the driver of the sedan that had picked me up outside of Derek Lance's house. The guy looked absolutely terrified, and as soon as his carefully prepared statement was read, he practically sprinted away from the microphones. I smiled. The bad guys were all gone or going into hiding. Operation Songbird was finished.

And, hey, if we'd not only put an end to the PB&J army but to their music career too, well, that was just icing on the cake.

I was sitting on the curb with Kyle, waiting for our parents to come pick us up. We hadn't said a word since we realized we'd survived the explosion, but there were enough fire trucks, news crews, and onlookers to do all the talking for us.

It still didn't seem fully real. That just the other day

I watched as vans carrying Derek Lance and his family pulled up to the abandoned home next to ours, and today I'd been fighting Derek in the middle of a cheesy robot pop-star army miles underground. It felt like I'd somehow fallen into a video game and survived the ending but had the bumps and bruises to show for it.

"What's gonna happen now?" Kyle asked.

"I have no idea. Who knows if they'll even find Le Carré's cave. They might just chalk it up to some sort of venti coffee meltdown."

"Yeah. I figured one of those was bound to happen someday. What happened to the girl?"

"I don't know," I said. "I don't know."

Just then we saw a small, furry animal scamper through the woods. It stopped to stare at us, gnashing its teeth once before disappearing into the forest.

"There goes Higgins," Kyle said.

"Guess we're not the only ones who made it out of there alive," I replied.

"No," he said. "I guess not."

I heard tires squeal up to the curb. Two cars stopped, and three people got out of them. Kyle's mom and dad—who were each well over six feet tall—and my own dad. Kyle's parents gathered him up into a gigantic, freakishly tall hug. My dad walked over to me. Tears were in his eyes. Something lead fell into my gut. I didn't wait for him to get to me. I got up, ran over to him, and threw my arms around him.

"It's okay, son," he said. "I'm here, Zeke. Nothing's going to happen to you."

"I know," I said, drooling tears and snot into his jacket. "Love you, Dad."

He took my face in his hands, smiled, and we continued hugging.

A police officer took statements from Kyle and me as witnesses. We told him we'd just hitchhiked over here, taken a joyride, and happened to see the whole mess go down. The officer gave us his card and told us to call him at the station if we remembered anything else. I told him we would.

I got into the car with my dad. Kyle and I shared a slight smile before our respective cars drove away.

Before Dad pulled out onto the highway, we sat there in silence for a while.

Finally he turned to me and said, "You sure you're all right, Zeke?"

"I'm fine, Dad. Just looking forward to getting home, getting back to my boring old life."

He patted me on the cheek. "We can do that."

I didn't really believe what I'd said. Though I was looking forward to getting home, I knew the adventures with Sparrow had changed me forever. I felt like I was a different Zeke. Same body, new motor.

When we got home, I passed right out and didn't wake up until the alarm clock woke me the next morning.

"Zeke!" my dad shouted. "Time for school!"

Funny. I had almost forgotten about school after everything that had happened. I dragged myself out of bed. It was only when I stood up that I realized how sore my body was. I guess with all the adrenaline that had been pumping through it the past few days, my body hadn't had a chance to really process all the abuse I'd put it through. Of course, not having really been very active before this didn't help. Like taking a rusty bicycle and trying to go from zero to ninety in thirty seconds.

When the school bus pulled up, I stumble-walked over and made my way up the steps. I found a seat and sighed as I lowered myself into it. A minute later, Kyle ambled on board. He was limping slightly. He made his way to the back and sat down next to me.

"I feel like I got run over by a truck," Kyle said.

"I feel like your truck attacked me when it was done with you."

"Your backpack looks light. No gadgets to bring to homeroom today?"

"Nah," I said. "I'm done with all that. Look where it got me."

"Yeah. You owe me a bit of an explanation," he said with a hint of annoyance.

"You'll get it," I said. "I promise. Now, wake me when we get to school."

The day passed faster than I could have imagined. I did my best to pay attention in class, but my mind was elsewhere. I was thinking about what Sparrow and I had done. The lives we'd saved. That despite all the pain I was in now, and how many times I'd almost been killed, something about the adventures felt right. Like maybe there was a reason I was still alive. Maybe Derek Lance was wrong. Maybe this nerdy dog hadn't just gotten lucky. Maybe I was actually good at this.

Don't get ahead of yourself, I thought. *You're back to being just plain old Zeke Bartholomew, Seventh-Grade Loser.*

Sometimes I didn't like what my internal monologue had to say to me.

That afternoon, once the final bell had rung, I met Kyle and we trudged through the hall on the way to the bus back home. We were both still limping and aching, but I was more sad than anything. I felt like a world had opened up in front of me, a world I'd always dreamed about being a part of, and then just as quickly closed on my face.

I was just plain old Ezekiel Bartholomew. Time to get used to it.

We left the school, threading our way through dozens of kids chatting, fooling around, done for the day. I was looking forward to seeing my dad again, but that was all. Once that school bus door closed, it was back to the usual.

I saw the bus idling, waiting for us. I frowned and kept walking.

"Hey, uh, Zeke," Kyle said, nudging me in the arm, right on a big old bruise.

"Ow, easy, big guy. What's up?"

"Look."

I stared off to where Kyle was pointing. And there, standing beside the bus, wearing a skirt and button-down top and carrying a regular backpack, was Sparrow.

"Isn't that—?" Kyle said.

"It is." I jogged over to Sparrow. A smile beamed across my face. I couldn't say the same for her; she looked as though her clothes might have well been made out of wasp stingers.

"I don't know how you people can wear things like this every day," Sparrow said.

"What do you mean? They're just clothes."

"Ugh, regular fibers are like wearing chicken wire. I'd go crazy if I had to wear wretched things like this every day."

"I don't know, I guess we just do."

"Well, until you've worn a uniform made out of Certivan fibers, you don't know what comfortable is."

"Certivan fibers?" I asked.

"It's what all SNURP uniforms are made from. Most comfortable, elastic, and breathable material in the world. Feels like you're wearing tissue paper, only it weighs less and can deflect small arms fire. Costs about twenty thousand dollars a suit."

"Wow," I said. "Where can I get one of those suits?"

"You can't," Sparrow said. She waited a moment, then added, "Unless you're a member of SNURP."

I sighed. "A boy can dream."

I toed the ground, not sure of what to say. I was glad to see Sparrow again, but it also reminded me of all the adventures I would never have.

"So what do you say, Zeke?" she said.

"What do you mean, what do I say?"

"Well, when I got back to HQ yesterday, I filled my bosses in on the kid who was responsible for saving the world. For taking down Le Carré and Ragnarok and preventing millions of kids from getting brainwashed by those PB&J drones."

"Yeah," I said. "You did a great job. The world owes you a debt of gratitude."

"Not me, stupid. You." She jabbed her thumb into yet another one of my bruises. (I swear, they must have been glowing or something.)

"Muh…muh…me?" I stammered.

"Yes, you, stupid."

"I don't understand," I said, feeling like my heart was on fire. "Why me?"

"Well," Sparrow answered, scratching at her clothing like it contained live insects. "You can't fight. You're not very skilled with traditional weaponry."

"Duly noted," I said under my breath.

"You're not very big. You're not very strong. And you don't run very fast."

"Okay, if you're just going to insult me..."

"But what you *do* have," Sparrow said, "is resolve. You have an incredible resilience that I haven't seen in many SNURP trainees. Much of the other things we can teach. We can teach you how to fight. How to disarm. How to disappear. How to evade capture. But you cannot teach someone heart. And that is why we want you to join us."

I smiled. My heart was beating like a hummingbird's wings. I didn't know what to say.

"Now, think about this before you say anything. If you accept," Sparrow said, "your life will never be the same. You will receive training that will test every fiber of your being. You will be challenged physically and mentally to degrees you never thought possible. You will say goodbye to your old life and begin a new one."

"Wait," I said, narrowing my eyes. "Are you saying—?"

"I've been given authorization to make you an offer to join the elite SNURP training program. Only the best and brightest kids from all over the world are asked to join. You will become a trainee in the most elite spy program in the world. You've proven yourself worthy this one time, Zeke. Now, are you willing to prove it the rest of your life?"

"Wait, are you serious?" I said.

"Do you see the clothes I'm wearing?" Sparrow said. "Do you *think* I would put on such awful clothes if I didn't have a job to do? You proved yourself resourceful. You have a lot of work to do, Zeke, if you say yes. Well, what's your answer?"

I didn't say a word, but instead threw my arms around Sparrow and gave her the biggest hug of my life. She pushed away from me, coughed, and smoothed out her clothing.

"Rule number one: no hugging in SNURP. You will act professional."

"Yes, ma'am."

Sparrow handed me a card. There was an address written on it.

"One month from today you will arrive at this address at exactly nine o'clock in the morning. Your school year will be finished. You will tell your father you've gotten a scholarship to the Camp Crystal Lagoon summer camp. We will provide all necessary paperwork and documentation to back up your claim."

"I'll be there," I said.

"Your training will start then."

"I can't wait."

Sparrow put out her hand. I looked at it, then shook it.

"You do know that you destroyed SirEebro, a piece of equipment valued at close to a billion dollars."

I gulped. "Um, are they going to bill me or something?"

Sparrow smiled. "Not literally. But I'm sure Master Zhen will make you pay for it in training.

"Master Zhen?"

"You'll meet him soon. He'll teach you fighting techniques that have saved my life dozens of times. Provided you don't mind having every one of your limbs bent like a pretzel."

"I, um, can't wait."

Sparrow nodded at me respectfully. "Good luck, Sea Otter."

"Sea otter?" I said, confused.

"The day you begin your training, you will be given the rank of sea otter."

"Um, not exactly the most dangerous or intimidating animal. Can't we go with polar bear or wombat or something?"

"That's the point. You start at the very bottom of the food chain. You might have done well this time, Zeke, but a SNURP agent does not rest on his laurels. You begin as a sea otter. Warm and cuddly. As you prove yourself, you will rise through the ranks. You will become more skilled. More dangerous. And then, only then, will you be feared."

"And then maybe I get ditch the whole sea otter thing. What rank are you?" I asked.

Sparrow just smiled. "Enjoy the rest of the school year, Zeke. Be ready. Keep it a secret. Even from your closest friends and family. You have no idea what you're in for."

Then Sparrow began to walk away.

"Hey!" I called out. She turned around. "You never told me your name."

Sparrow just smiled and said, "One month, Bartholomew. Get ready."

I watched her as she crossed the street and disappeared.

Kyle joined me. I was still standing there, dumbstruck.

"What did she say?" he asked.

"Oh, uh, nothing. Just saying good-bye and thanks. She also told me how brave and handsome I am."

"You're lying."

"I am."

Kyle laughed. "Come on, Zeke. Back to our boring lives."

As we boarded the school bus, I said to Kyle, "You know, I'm thinking about going to summer camp this year."

THE END?

Two days later. Just a normal kid again. Sigh. Time for more meatloaf...

The school bus pulled up in front of my house. I said good-bye to Kyle and limped my way down the stairs. For some reason, my house looked newer. The colors brighter. The grass more inviting. This was the first day of the rest of my life.

My dad greeted me inside.

"Hey, Zeke, how was school?"

"Same old, same old."

"That's nice. Hey, you know that family that just moved in next door? You know, the old Wickersham place?"

I turned to him, hesitant. "Yeah…"

"Well, they're gone already."

"Really?"

"Yeah. A bunch of vans pulled up this morning, took everything but the kitchen sink out, and left. Guess the place wasn't what they thought it would be."

I looked out the window. All the security cameras were gone. There was no sign of life. "No. I guess not."

"Oh, well. One less neighbor to borrow sugar from."

"Hey, Dad?"

"Yes, Zeke?"

"I was thinking about going to summer camp this year."

My dad smiled. "I think that's a great idea. Experience the outdoors. Have some adventures. What brought this on?"

"Oh, nothing," I said dreamily. "Just about time I start living."

"Well, I'm all in favor. We can talk about it later."

"Thanks, Dad."

"Oh, and, Zeke, somebody dropped this off for you today."

He handed me a small package, crudely wrapped. There was nothing written on it except for my name in large Magic Marker.

"I'm gonna go read a book. Glad you're home, son."

"Thanks, Dad."

My heart was bursting out of my chest. It was from Sparrow, I knew it. Information about SNURP and my summer camp cover.

I tore open the package, unable to contain my joy with what I would find.

Only there were no pamphlets inside. There was an item inside the package.

My mouth went dry as I removed it. Looked at it. Turned it over in my hands. I knew exactly what it was, and who it was from.

Inside the package was a pair of broken sunglasses. And attached to the sunglasses was a note with six simple words that made my blood run cold:

You're going to pay for these. —D. L.

The adventure continues in

ZEKE BARTHOLOMEW
AND THE SUMMER CAMP OF DOOM

PAGE 1

Zeke: Put on the sunglasses I have enclosed in the envelope.

PAGE 2

Zeke: The sunglasses you are currently wearing are optically tailored to your genetic makeup. The page you are reading right now can only be viewed while wearing these glasses, and to anyone else they will appear in look and function like any ordinary cheap sunglasses. Still, your discretion cannot be overstated.

Starting June 15, you will begin your training. It will not be easy. We will test your mind, your body, and your spirit in ways you cannot imagine. You have been chosen to participate in this program with some of the most talented young spy prodigies in the entire world. Your success depends on your ability to function both as an individual and as part of a group.

You will be picked up at 10:00 a.m. Eastern Standard Time on the morning of June 15. Your transportation will appear as an ordinary school bus. But I assure you, there is nothing ordinary about it.

Your front is that you will be attending summer camp, specifically Camp Crystal Lagoon in New Hampshire. This camp does not exist, but we have created a facade that will quell doubts of any parents or friends. You are required to pack clothing, accessories, and toiletries as though you will be attending summer camp. None of these articles will come into use during your training; they merely add to your cover as a camper. All clothing and equipment will be provided to you by SNURP at the appropriate times during your training.

We are eager to begin your training, Zeke Bartholomew. As I have stated, you will begin with the rank of Sea Otter. As you progress in your career, your title will grow as you do. Stay smart. Stay safe. And get ready for the ride of your life.

Sincerely,
Sparrow

When you end the school year saving the world from an evil mastermind bent on world domination while nearly getting blown to bits in a hundred different ways, what do you do during the summer between seventh and eighth grade? Well in my case, you go to summer camp.

Okay, that's not entirely true. You see, going to summer camp was the cover story I had to tell my dad and all my friends at school (namely Kyle Quint, who was pretty much my only friend). According to the story, I would be spending close to three months at Camp Crystal Lagoon, a bucolic place nestled in the peaceful woods of New Hampshire. At Crystal Lagoon, I would learn arts and crafts, play handball, go rock climbing, and sit around campfires making s'mores. Yup, a pretty normal summer for a twelve-year-old.

Only none of it was true.

The truth of the matter is that I wasn't going to summer camp. Camp Crystal Lagoon didn't exist beyond a website and some professional-looking brochures, full of smiling kids and happy counselors. Where I was really going for the summer was a matter of national security. Seriously.

After I saved the world (yeah, I had to say it again, because, hey, it sounds pretty cool to say), I was offered a spot as an official trainee of the secret spy organization SNURP, which stands for Strategic National Underground Reconnaissance Project. SNURP is a top-secret spy agency, and one of their top spies, a girl my age named Sparrow, who'd helped me save the world (I'm never going to get tired of that), asked if I would take part.

She told me it would be like nothing I'd ever experienced. That my mind and body would be pushed to the breaking point. That there would be days I'd wish I'd never been born and nights where I'd cry for home. So, naturally, I said yes.

You see, I've always been something of a dreamer. Up until a few months ago, the most exciting moment of my life was accidentally setting my underwear on fire during a terrible Bunsen burner accident during science class. But that all changed.

I'm not a kid anyone would describe as special. I'm not

that tall and not especially athletic; I have reddish brown hair that looks like the victim of a particularly nasty weed whacker; and I often get picked for sports teams after inanimate objects like mops and cleaning supplies. Yet for some reason Sparrow saw something in me, and invited me to go away for the summer to see if I had what it took to become a real spy.

So right now I'm sitting in my room at 5 Sunnyvale Drive, packing heaps of clothing and accessories into a duffel bag to take with me to SNURP headquarters. I don't know where the headquarters is, but I was instructed by Sparrow to bring clothing and personal effects that one might take to summer camp. Not that I would be needing my iPod or an e-reader or comic books or a stationary set, but I had to give the impression that I really was going away for summer camp.

I was scheduled to be picked up in ten minutes, so I was double-checking to make sure I had everything I didn't need. There was a knock at my door.

"Come in," I said.

The door pushed inward, and my dad stood there. He was wearing tattered jeans and a T-shirt. There was a smile on his face that was a mixture of pride and sadness.

"Almost done packing?" he asked. "The bus should be here any minute."

"Just about," I replied, pounding the duffel so I could close it. My dad stepped into the room. He put his hand on my shoulder.

"Can't believe you're going away for so long," he said. "But I'm glad you're going. This will be good for you. Get away, get in touch with nature, meet some new friends."

"Yeah. Nature." I couldn't tell my dad that instead of studying trees I would likely spend most mornings being beaten to a pulp by Sparrow and the SNURP staff. But I felt good. I'd actually been exercising, to train for this day. I'd gotten up to three miles on the treadmill—not too shabby for someone who used to get out of breath carrying his lunch tray twenty feet. This was a day I'd literally dreamed about my whole life. The chance to do something great. Or at least try to do something great before failing miserably.

"I'm gonna miss you, Zeke," my dad said.

"Aw, come on, Dad, I'll be back. And I'll write."

"You'd better," he said, laughing.

I loved my dad more than anything. Ever since my mom died when I was five, we were all we had. He devoted his life to providing a home for me, for being there for me. I think he'd dated here and there, but I think he saw us as a unit, a family, and never wanted to put anyone ahead of me. Including himself.

"Have fun this summer, Dad," I said. "Go, like, dancing or something."

"Dancing?" he asked.

"I don't know, what do old people do for fun?"

"Oh, so I'm old now?" he said, messing with my hair, which I think actually made it look better. "I'll be fine. You be safe. And wear bug spray. I got Lyme disease once and it was no picnic."

"Wear bug spray. Check. Thanks, Dad."

He simply smiled. I wasn't sure what to say. This would be the longest I'd gone without seeing my dad in my whole life. And for some reason, I was just as worried about him as he was about me.

A horn blared outside. We checked the window. A long, yellow school bus was parked outside of our driveway. I could see dozens of faces of young kids peering out. Talking. Laughing. Were these the other SNURP trainees? Sure seemed like there were a lot of them.

"Come on, Zeke," my dad said. "Let's see you off."

He went to pick up my duffel, but I stopped him. "I got it."

"Of course," he said. "Keep forgetting you're not a little kid anymore."

We went downstairs and outside. My dad walked me to the end of the driveway. The school bus door opened. The driver was a bored-looking man who didn't even bother to look at me. I could hear all the other kids. I wondered who they were. What their gifts were. How I would fit in.

"Good-bye, son," my dad said. "You're not too old to give your dad a hug, are you?"

"Of course not." I wrapped my arms around my father and squeezed him tight. I heard him choke back a sob. Then I let go and boarded the bus to my destiny.

The door closed behind me, and the bus peeled off. I walked down the aisle looking for a seat. Strangely, none of the kids seemed to notice me or pay me any attention. Did I smell strange or something?

Then, something really strange happened...

When we rounded the corner, there was an electronic humming sound and all the kids disappeared. Like, there one second, gone the next. I was alone on the bus. I turned back to ask the driver what was going on…but there was no driver. The bus was operating automatically. The kids and the driver were an electrical projection to keep up appearances.

"Whoa…" I muttered.

"*Ezekiel J. Bartholomew*," a voice said. I recognized it. Sparrow. "*Sit down anywhere.*"

I slid into the nearest seat. The moment I sat down, a small screen opened in front of me, and a video began to play.

On the screen was Sparrow. She looked just like the last time I'd seen her. Strong, wiry, bold, and brave. With steely blue eyes and auburn hair pulled back in a ponytail. She was wearing a rubbery-looking suit with the letters SNURP sewn into the chest.

She spoke.

"You are here because you've been chosen to be a part of the most elite young spy trainee program in the world. Do not take it lightly. You will learn more in due time. These are the fellow members of your team. They will be your competition and your backup. You will get to know them better than you know your best friends."

On the screen appeared a boy. Only this didn't look

like any boy I'd ever seen. He stood about six feet tall, with bright blond hair and a chiseled face. He had muscles in places I didn't even think I had places. The video showed him lifting free weights the size of my dad's car.

"This is Thor Knudson," Sparrow said. "Thor was born with a rare genetic mutation called myostatin, which doubles its owner's muscle mass. Thor is from Oslo, Norway, and is the strongest kid in the world."

The video showed Thor being awarded a gold medal, while other, slightly less-muscular kids looked on in disappointment. I gulped.

Then, a video came on showing a young girl. She was tall, lithe, dark haired, and olive skinned, wearing shorts and a tank top. She was standing in the middle of what looked like a giant obstacle course.

"This is Laila Mansour. Born in Marrakesh, Morocco, Laila has secured her own prominent title."

Just like that, Laila swung up onto a pair of high beams, and proceeded to flip, flop, and glide through the air like her body was made of rubber. She was like a combination bird, frog, leopard, and one of those rubber bouncy balls. Then, she literally did a backflip, springing off a wall, and landed on her feet.

"Laila Mansour is known as the Princess of Parkour."

Sparrow's voice continued to narrate as I was introduced to the rest of my fellow SNURP trainees. I met Henry Chang from San Francisco, who was trained in every martial art known to man. The Ninja. Alexi Pontneuffe from Monte Carlo, who could blend into any environment. The Chameleon. And lastly I met Astrid Ingall from Mozambique, South Africa. She could pick up any scent, follow any lead, and find anyone, anywhere. The Tracker.

And lastly, a picture came on the screen end the presentation. I recognized it. It was my fifth grade yearbook photo. I had braces. I had the worst haircut in the history of bad haircuts. And there was a hole in my sweater from when I snagged it on the handle of Mr. Statler's homeroom.

"This is Ezekiel Bartholomew," Sparrow said. "Looks can be deceiving. Zeke is a master inventor, able to use infrared technology, fiber optics, and household items to create items that are necessary in any tactical mission."

I'm pretty sure my face turned bright red—but it made me smile.

Sparrow came on the screen again.

"This is your team. You will meet them in person very soon.

"Now, search the seat pocket in front of you. You will find a small, wrapped pill and a bottle of water."

I stuck my hand into the pocket, came out with the water and a tiny white pill.

"Swallow the pill. Wash it down. And I'll see you soon."

I stared at the pill.

"Here goes nothing," I said. I unwrapped it, popped it in my mouth, and took a swig of water.

Seconds later, my head felt woozy. One minute later, I was out like a light, my adventure about to begin.

ACKNOWLEDGMENTS

Even though books are written alone, they are never published alone. So Zeke and I have a lot of people to thank for making this book come to life.

First I have to thank my agent, Joe Veltre, who championed the idea for Zeke's adventures before I'd written a single word on the page. If Zeke ever decides to write his own books, Joe is the guy he should approach. And if Joe has any sense, he'll turn Zeke down. I don't want him stealing my spotlight.

The team at Sourcebooks has been incredible every step of the way, and I owe them thanks for their vision, expertise, and exquisite fashion sense. Massive thanks go to Todd Stocke, Kelly Barrales-Saylor, Aubrey Poole, and Dominique Raccah. I bow down to my fantastic and patient editor, Rebecca Frazer, as well as my copyeditors, Kristin Zelazko and Jill Hughes. I also owe

Daniel Ehrenhaft tremendous gratitude for bringing Zeke to Sourcebooks Jabberwocky. If Zeke had any musical talent, he'd definitely audition for Tiger Beat. But he doesn't, so that's a moot point.

My family, as always, has given me the love and support every growing boy needs, and I can't thank them enough. I'd like to thank Wilson, my dog, even though he tried his hardest to delay the writing of this book. You try writing a thousand words a day with a small, furry dog constantly trying to climb up into your lap.

I'm a book lover deep down to my core, and my thanks go out to all booksellers and librarians who have expressed enthusiasm for Zeke. You are the gatekeepers to the best stories ever created.

Most of all, I want to thank all the kids (and adults!) who read Zeke's adventures. I wrote this book because it was the kind of story that enraptured me as a child. I hope my joy and love of adventure shines through on these pages. It's all of you who made me want to create Zeke, and I hope you enjoy many more of his adventures for years to come.

ABOUT THE AUTHOR

Jason Pinter is the author of five thriller novels with 1.5 million copies in print in many languages, nearly all of which he cannot understand. His first novel, *The Mark*, was optioned to be a major motion picture, but Steven Spielberg has stopped returning his calls. He has also been nominated for numerous awards—and lost every one. He tells people that it is an honor just to be nominated, but silently wishes he could have won just one of them. He lives in New York City with his dog, Wilson, who constantly has to dig him out from under a pile of books. This is Jason's first book for young readers. You can learn more at www.jasonpinter.com, email him at jason@jasonpinter.com, or follow his every random thought on Twitter at twitter.com/jasonpinter.